Lock Down Publications and Ca$h
Presents

I0680404

KILLA KOUNTY

Part 5

The Bloody Godmother

Written By

Khufu

First Edition 2024

Printed in the United States of America

Lock Down Publications
P.O. Box 944
Stockbridge, GA 30281
www.lockdownpublications.com

Like our page on Facebook: Lock Down Publications
www.facebook.com/lockdownpublications.ldp

Stay Connected with Us!

Text **LOCKDOWN** to 22828 to stay up-to-date with new releases, sneak peaks, contests and more…

Like our page on Facebook:
Lock Down Publications

Join Lock Down Publications/The New Era Reading Group

Visit our website:
www.lockdownpublications.com

Follow us on Instagram:
Lock Down Publications

Email Us: We want to hear from you!

Acknowledgements

The edginess of my humor is provoked by a life lived on the edge. Through all my years, I've managed to survive overwhelming circumstances through guile, militancy, and the will of "The Most High!" Being able to take a multitude of experiences to formulate words into a vivid narrative is a challenge, and I acknowledge "The Most High" for instilling in me, the ability to channel tragedy, pain, and rage into an art…For it is not a simple task. I also acknowledge the big homie Cash for drafting me to the winning team. LDP over everything! To my fans, I love you dearly! Shout out to my nigga Bats from New York and everybody who woopin; Thats Double R! Shout out to my crip, vice lords, ocks, G.D and homies! And most importantly… I salute the big homie Kream! A.M.G. shit! Militant we stand!

Dedication

I dedicate this book to Stacy, Tela, Tayda, Lanetta, and all who were injured and killed in the MLK massacre in Fort Pierce. Fla.

FREE DA REAL

Free Quinten Bradly, Jimmy Reeves, Rock, Tray, Keedy Trini, Jihad, Bats and D-Zoe.

QUOTE

Nothing or none is immune to the entropy of the universe.

Chapter 1
WHOLE CLIP

"Wassup, Charity? How are you doin' today?" Ketta asked the forensic lab technician.

"I'm fine, but I'll be better when you let me take you out," Charity retorted, shooting her shot.

"Girrllll…! I done told your ass, I suck and fuck dick! I ain't into bumpin' coochies and shit," Ketta intoned fervently.

"You don't know wha'cha missing."

"I ain't missing shit. Na, knock it off and tell me wassup with them results," said Ketta somewhat irritated.

"Okay, bitch, damn. They came back today. The DNA on the rag is a Khafre Moss, and the blood belonged to a Husain Moss. Does that help any?"

"Um, yeah. Thank you, Charity. I'll call you later." Ketta hung up and placed two fingers on her temple. After retrieving the red rag that Khafre had gotten from the voodoo priest, Ketta had her friend at the lab run tests before giving it back to Khafre. He had told her that he'd killed his son Husain for attempting to tell on Tasha, but she wanted clarity.

"Damn, Khafre," Ketta mumbled before falling into deep thought.

Boc!

A gunshot and a policeman running into Wolly's store shook Ketta out of her contemplative state.

"Assata!" Ketta screamed, grabbing her service weapon and heading in the store. Once in the store, Ketta was frightened and confused at what she saw.

"Drop, your fucking, weapon! Last chance!" Warned the rookie cop.

"Assata, please. Put the gun down," Wolly pleaded.

"Assata, put it down, baby," Ketta instructed, pointing the weapon at the rookie cop, prepared to kill him if he shot Assata.

"Who the fuck are you?" The cop asked noting Ketta's weapon out of his peripheral.

"I'm a detective! Everybody just calm down and lower your weapons," demanded Ketta.

"Fuck no!" Rookie cop retorted, visibly shaking.

"Assata, I have everything on tape. You killed him in self-defense. Everything will be okay. Please, put the gun down," begged Wolly.

Ketta looked at the dead man on the floor slumped, then gazed at Assata concerningly. "Assata, please!" Cried Ketta.

Assata looked at the cop with blood in her eyes then dropped the gun. The cop rushed Assata and detained her aggressively.

"You okay, baby?" Asked Ketta.

"Yeah, I'm good. I shoulda put the whole clip in his ass!"

***

Khafre sat dubiously as he contemplated his situation and listened to his captors speak with foreign dialect. He noted that neither of their attire bore any title of the Alphabet Boyz; no Feds, DEA, or ATF...Nothing! Since his capture, his captors surprisingly weren't aggressive or trying to cause him any harm which Khafre found peculiar. If it wasn't the Feds, jack boyz, or hitman...who the fuck was it? Khafre's thoughts were all over the place when a captor that sat behind him placed a nylon bag over his head.

"What the fuck my nigga?" yelled Khafre.

Another captor injected a tranquilizer of some sort into Khafre's arm. Moments later, it was lights out.

Five hours later, Khafre awoke a bit drowsy and in a disoriented state. What lay before him persuaded him to believe that he was hallucinating. Hallucination or not, tears fell from the wells of Khafre's eyes irresistibly.

"Wassup wit' it, King?"

Chapter 2
STANK AS FUCK!
Four years later...

"Bitch, I can't believe you just did a whole bid for killin' a nigga," Tasha stated, passing Assata the blunt.

"What's so unbelievable about that?" Assata implored before taking a pull of the blunt.

"You was fourteen, like...What the fuck?" Tasha retorted, waving her hands in a feminine gesture.

"So what age bracket I gotta be in for a motherfucka to respect me? Huh? That pussy ass nigga disrespected me, so, I put 'em down. You sleep if you think that was my first rodeo. I'm from Killa Kounty. Where you from? Port St. Lucie?" Assata snapped.

"Don't play wit' me. I'm Loose County's finest! The city of no pity, baby," Tasha retorted full of animation. "And why you takin' shit personally? I was just saying, you was a lil' young when you did that."

Assata waved Tasha off. "Yeah, whatever, man," Assata exclaimed. After killing Pooh Daddy, Assata was sentenced to juvenile life and was to be released once she turned 18 years of age. She served four years in Ocala, Florida's Women's Reception Center and was now back in the streets of Killa Kounty.

"So, how long you been home?" Tasha questioned, trying to lighten the tension.

"I been out a month," Assata retorted dryly then made a right on Airport Road.

"Where are we headed?" Asked Tasha.

"I'm finna pull up on my loud man, 'cause you got a bitch smokin' straight pooch."

"This shit smoking. I got this from my lil' snack for free-free."

"I see why," said Assata, making another right on Seneca Avenue. "Hand me my vape pen. It's on yo' side, in the door," Assata asked Tasha.

"You sho' it ain't on yo' side, 'cause I'on see it," pronounced Tasha. When Tasha looked back, she noticed that Assata had spit something into her right hand. By the time Tasha could comprehend what it was, Assata had already swiped the Gem Star Razor across her face twice. "Assata!" Tasha yelled as the left side of her jaw opened up. Tasha's teeth could be seen as clear as day. She grabbed her face then glanced at her bloody hand. Blood dripped relentlessly from her face as the pain set in. "Aaaahhhh!" Tasha yelled then attempted to jump out of the car, but Assata had the doors on child safety lock.

"N'all, pussy hoe! Don't scream, na!" Assata snapped, swiping the razor across Tasha's face, head, arms, and any flesh that she left open.

"Aaaaahhh! What did I do? Plleeeaasse! Stop!" Cried Tasha, shaking violently.

Assata threw the razor at her, then grabbed a Styrofoam cup from the console that was full of piss and threw it on Tasha.

"Bitch, you was stupid enough to get in this car with me after posting that shit about my brother Husain!" Assata snatched her Glock 31 from the side of her door and pointed it at Tasha's face. "You put on Facebook my brother is a snitch! My bloodline doesn't breed rats!"

"I promise you! His ass was finna tell on meeee!" Tasha cried.

"Bitch, where the paperwork? Show me that in black and white!"

"I don't have it on me!"

"Exactly!"

Boc! Boc! Boc!

Assata put three in Tasha's head and made a U-Turn, headed back towards Taylor's Creek. Assata didn't know that Husain was going to assist the government against Tasha in a murder case before he died. When she was in prison, Assata had a phone and was able to see what Tasha posted about Husain. She made it her business to bake Tasha a cake. While in deep thought, an odious smell flooded the vehicle, Tasha's bowels had loosened up, causing her to defecate and piss on herself.

"Damn, hoe…You stank as fuck!" Assata stated as she made her way to Taylor's Creek and dumped the murder bucket into the murky waters.

Chapter 3
LIABILITY

Assata entered the house slightly enhanced from the day's events. The only thing on her mind was taking a shower and catching a power nap. On the way to her room, she bumped into Ketta who was coming out of her bathroom.

"Excuse me, baby. I didn't even hear you come in," Ketta apologized, patting Assata's shoulder.

"It's okay, ma." Assata had started calling Ketta ma during her last two years in prison. Ketta had been there for her mentally and financially. This compelled Assata to have an undeniable love for her. Assata would bring Ketta the moon if asked.

"You hungry?" Ketta asked, noting the blood splatter on Assata's tight fitted Elder Statesman tie-dye sweat suit.

"No, ma'am. I just want to jump in the shower and lay it down."

Ketta lifted Assata's chin with her index finger. "You aight?" Ketta asked, knowing Assata had just put somebody down.

"Yes, ma'am," retorted Assata mildly.

Ketta kissed Assata on the forehead. "Okay baby. Make sure you get rid of these clothes." Ketta went to her room and Assata did the same.

In deep thought, Assata let the steamy hot water run through her dreads and trickle down her curvaceous frame. Standing 5'5", Assata had the perfect size C-cup breasts, a flat stomach, and a deep arch in her back that led to her perfect, firm posterior. Her hazel eyes and deep dimples alone captivated anyone who encountered her. Assata was indubitably beautiful. Thirty minutes later, she stepped out of the shower, got herself together, then laid back in her queen size bed.

Just as she was dozing off, Hassan rolled through her door in his wheelchair. He'd climbed out of a coma, but he was a paraplegic.

"Wassup, killa? Get'cha ass sup!" Hassan exclaimed, pulling from a blunt and handing it to Assata.

"Come on, man. I'm trying to sleep," she whined, throwing a pillow at Hassan who caught it and threw it back.

"I ain't tryna hear that shit! Sleep when a nigga kill you," Hassan stated, attempting to pass Assata the blunt again.

"These niggaz, ain't smart enough to kill me," she pronounced, grabbing the blunt and inhaling it.

"Talk that shit, then." Hassan smiled. "So wassup? Where you was at?"

"Handling bidness."

"What kinda bidness?"

Assata inhaled, then exhaled before speaking. "I had to put Tasha under," Assata pronounced; voice cultured but cruel.

"Whatchu mean?" Asked Hassan, reaching for the blunt.

"Tasha. I took her down. I killed that hoe."

"For what?" Hassan asked, eyebrows creased.

"You seen that shit she put on Facebook 'bout Husain?"

"Yeah, I seen that shit."

"Okay, then. Our bloodline don't breed rats! She violated."

"I hear you, but damn! You couldn't just beat the hoe ass?"

"I'm way past that. I'on do no fighting. I'm booking tickets to the graveyard," Assata declared, flashing a devilish grin.

"You know I'm fuckin' her cousin Lee Lee, right?" Hassan asked, passing the blunt back to Assata.

"Yeah, I know. I might have to put her down, too," Assata proclaimed, blowing out a cloud of smoke.

"For what?"

"She might know that I was the last one wit' Tasha." Assata passed the blunt back.

"N'all, sis, I can't let'chu do that."

"Fuck you mean? You choosing pussy over my freedom?" Assata sat up and planted both feet on the floor.

Hassan exhaled deeply. "It ain't that, lil' sis. When you was in prison and I was laid up in that bed, she was there for me. When I pissed and shitted on myself, she cleaned and bathed me. You hear me? She cleaned the shit off me! That's a real bitch."

"That shit cute or whateva, but I ain't tryna hear none of that shit! Anybody can get it! Anybody!" Assata stated, looking Hassan in his eyes, letting him know that he wasn't exempt from her wrath.

Hassan caught the underlying threat but decided not to feed into it. He loved his little sister vehemently, and would never war with her. Hassan took another pull of the blunt before replying, "Look, sis, I ain't gon' cap. I got love for Lee Lee, but not as much love as I harbor for you. Wit' that being said, if she becomes a problem, I'll deal with it," Hassan assured.

"Aight na. I love your ass, too, but boy…!"

"I got it, sis. On Husain, I got it."

"Okay."

"Everything, aight in here?" Ketta asked, peeking her head in Assata's room.

"Yeah, ma, everything velvet," assured Assata.

"Yeah. I'm in here if y'all need me," Ketta stated before leaving.

"So wassup?" Hassan hit then passed the blunt to Assata.

"What'chu mean?"

"I'm tryna spin on some shit," pronounced Hassan, referring to killing someone.

Assata smirked. "I heard you were spinnin' on shit while I was away."

"Yeah, I put a few niggas under, but them niggas took my legs from me, forever. So, I'm spinnin' on them niggas *foreva!*" Hassan declared warily.

"How the hell you was pullin' drive-bys with no legs?" Assata questioned curiously.

"Lee-Lee. Every time I slid on niggaz, Lee Lee was there assisting me. That's why I fuck wit' her. Loyalty is everything."

"Yeah, she is loyal to you now, but how loyal she will she remain if them crackers tell her she is facing life? Huh? Now, she really is a liability 'cause this bitch knows everybody you killed. Don't ever give a bitch accolades if she ain't never been up under that pressure. You trippin', brah," Assata informed, slightly angered that Hassan would put such trust into someone after all he's been through.

"I hear wha'chu, spittin'. You're right, and I'ma deal wit' it accordingly if need be."

"Say less. You know we all we got."

"Already! Na, can we spin on some shit? Damn!"

Chapter 4
LET THE SONG PLAY

It was a little after twelve in the afternoon when Assata made her way down 13th Street. As she neared the Blue Store, a group of niggaz could be seen kicking it, all dressed in white t-shirts, blue jeans, and blue Jordan One retro hightops. All rivals had to take caution when passing by the Blue Store. Everybody was always strapped and paid close attention to every vehicle that passed. Assata and Hassan knew this but didn't give a fuck.

"Look at these goofy ass niggaz, sis. It's like Duck Hunt out this mothafucka!" Hassan announced excitedly.

"I view that," Assata retorted. "You ready?"

"Already!" Pronounced Hassan gripping his .223 pistol.

The Blue Store was close to the street, making its occupants an easy target. Assata wore a ski mask, but Hassan was barefaced. He wanted his opps to see his face. Assata casually pulled in front of the store, staring at the young killaz. They all clutched their pistols but did not fire. Behind the 5 percent tint, EST GEE'S *If I Stop Now* could be heard bleeding from the sound system.

I hold my gun/ more than I hold my son/
No way in hell/ you catch me without one/
I been in war. More than I been in love/
We in them carz/alnight till morning' come
Hunnid on me now/
Somebody call my bluff...

Assata placed the tip of her AK 47 against the window while one of them attempted to peek inside the whip. She turned her face from the window and squeezed a shot off, shattering the window and blowing the youngin's face off. Hassan had dropped the back window and gave it to everybody that attempted to round the back of the store.

"Don't run na!" taunted Hassan who continued to fire upon his opps.

Assata hopped out of her whip and chased the known killaz into the store. She let the AK go, decimating everything in sight. 7.62 rounds tore through the chips rack and shelves that the youngins hid behind. Assata walked down all four Iles, waving the assault rifle, killing everybody in the store.

When she turned towards the door, the Arab owner had his pistol raised. He squeezed off a shot, but missed. This proved to be fatal. Assata sent lead his way, ripping his neck and chest open. Pickled egg and pig feet juice splattered about when rounds tore through their jars. Assata jogged out of the store and killed two innocent people who were walking by. She quickly hopped into the vehicle with Hassan and pulled off.

"Bitch ass niggaz!" Yelled Hassan.

Assata smiled, her adrenaline pumping from doing her first mission with her brother since being home. "Na, that's how you let the song play on them niggas!" Assata added, turning EST GEE up to the max.

***

Two Days Later...

"Where are we headed?" Hassan asked from the backseat.

"Somebody wanna see you," Ketta explained, pulling out of the gated community that she lived in.

"Somebody who? We ain't got no kinfolks. They all dead," Assata stated comically.

"And how is that funny?" Ketta asked, glancing at Assata concerningly before returning her attention back to the road in front of her.

"It's better than crying. Shid... Our people cursed. Dealing with my father, I'm sure you know that by now."

"Facts!" Added Hassan.

"Speakin' of my father, you heard anything? You know if they caught him or not? Is he even alive?" Assata questioned.

"He's not in federal custody, and I don't know if he's alive," Ketta pronounced dolefully.

"If he ain't in federal custody, he alive! I'm tellin' ya' what I know! I know my pops!" Hassan exclaimed, full of animation.

"Ion know 'bout that. It's been over five years. He wouldn't go that long without making contact," said Assata.

"See, that's the thing. When you running from them crackers, you can't make contact. You seen what happened to Pablo. Pop killed two federal agents. He can't never make contact," asserted Hassan.

"You right," Ketta admitted, pulling into Patty's seafood. "I miss the fuck outta him."

"Hell yeah!" Assata added.

"Listen, y'all. Wait here. I'll be back in a minute." Ketta got out of the car and headed inside the restaurant.

"What you think of Ketta?" questioned Assata as her phone started ringing.

"I love Ketta. She helped me a lot when I came outta that coma. Her and Lee Lee."

"Yeah, I love her too. And speaking of Lee Lee…" Assata stated answering the phone. "Wassup, Lee Lee?" Asked Assata, putting the phone speaker.

"Hey, girl," Lee Lee said dryly. "I'm calling to see if you seen Tasha."

"N'all, I ain't seen or heard from her. What's going on?"

"I'on know, but she has been missing for a few days. It ain't like her to not call. We talk every day. Her mother filed a missing person report. It's all over Facebook."

"Damn, that's crazy," exclaimed Assata.

"I know, 'cause she told me she was gonna get up with you before she left the house," Lee Lee informed.

Assata gave Hassan an all-knowing look. A look that stated, *You know what to do.* Hassan rubbed his hands through his dread and down his face. He dreaded his next move.

"Yeah, we was supposed to meet up, but she never came through. You sho' she ain't wit' no nigga?"

"N'all, she would've told me. Something ain't right, I can feel it."

"I'on think so. She'll pop out in a day or two. Listen, I gotta go, but keep me posted, aight?"

Lee Lee exhaled deeply before replying, "Yeah whatever!" She hung up.

Assata faced Hassan. "You know wha'chu gotta do, nigga!" Assata stated, somewhat threateningly.

"Yeah, man. Tsss…I got'cha," Hassan lamented.

"Hey, grandma babies!" Greeted Patty. She was Assata and Hassan's great-grandmother. It was her first time seeing them.

"Assata, Hassan, this is Mrs. Patty. She's your great-grandmother," Ketta informed.

Assata gazed at the beautiful elderly woman in admiration, then looked back at Hassan who was doing the same. Then, she exited the vehicle.

Patty approached Assata who had a single tear streaming down her right cheek and placed her hands on both sides of Assata's face.

"Grandma?" Assata spoke just above a whisper. She was taken aback, thinking that she and Hassan were the only family members left.

"I am." Patty wiped Assata's tears with her thumbs, and kissed Assata's forehead.

By this time, Ketta had helped Hasan out of the car. Assata buried her face in her grandmother's chest and held her tight.

"Wassup, grandma? Nice to meet'chu," Hassan said, rolling up in his wheelchair.

Assata finally unwrapped her arms from around Mrs. Patty.

"Hey, baby. You look just like yo' grandpappy and father," Patty stated, leaning down to hug and kiss Hassan on the cheek. She then gave Hassan a onceover before speaking again. "How did you get into a wheelchair?" Patty asked, already knowing the answer.

"I got caught up, G-Ma."

"The ones who did it still alive?"

"No, ma'am."

"Yeah, you most definitely yo' daddy's son."

"Have you heard from him?" asked Hassan.

Patty exhaled deeply. "I get calls all the time from different numbers. They were telling me that Khafre said to meet him here and there with the money. I didn't pay it no mind. I know it's the Feds."

"What if it's really him sending a message, grandma?" Assata inquired, building up hope in her mind.

"Trust me, baby, it's the Feds. Na, listen. The reason I got in contact with Ketta, for one, is because I wanted to see my great-grandbabies before I passed over. Secondly, I wanted to leave you and your brother a house. It's a three-bedroom, two-bath, and garage."

"Thank you, Grandma," said Assata, hugging her.

"Where the house at, G-Ma?" Questioned Hassan.

"It's actually down the street from where your father lived. It's on Avenue S."

"How come you never come by to see us?" Hassan questioned, frowning deeply.

Assata thought about what her father had told her regarding the history of the family.

"I always wondered the same about you all. I'm sure your father told you that I was close by, but that's neither here nor there. I just wanted to leave my grandbabies something before I leave.

"Where you goin'?" Hassan asked.

"*Africa.*"

Chapter 5
GOD IS A WOMAN

The sun had almost disappeared from the skyline when Assata pulled up to Wolly's brown store in Ketta's Benz. Assata noted the traffic was mild as she hopped out and headed inside the store. She saw that Wolly had a few customers so she waited patiently off to the side.

"Excuse me, Miss Lady," someone said.

Assata turned to see who was speaking to her and became short of breath. It felt like time had slowed down, as her observation of this God-like being downloaded in her mental catalog. Standing 5'7", his skin resembled black gold. His dreads were shoulder-length, thick and nappy, complimented by a razor-sharp tape line. He bore a baby face, but his eyes depicted an old soul—experience and pain. To top it off, he was tatted like the subway in Harlem, with the body of an African warrior.

"Miss lady?"

Assata snapped back to real time. "Yes?" Assata cleared her throat. "I mean, yah. Wassup?"

"I was askin' you if you believe in God."

"Shid, I do now," admitted Assata still gazing in his eyes.

"It's funny you say that, 'cause the moment you walked in this store, I stamped in my mind, that God gotta be a woman."

Assata smiled. "That shit was cute. How often do you use that line?"

"This was the first. You inspired that."

"Lucky me, huh?" Assata retorted.

"I'm G.I. Nice to meet'chu, Dimples." G.I. held his hand out.

"I'm Assata. Pleasure to meet you, too, Afrika," replied Assata.

"We giving nicknames out and we ain't exchanged numbers yet?"

"You ain't gettin' my number, boy. You smooth, but not that smooth," Assata stated before walking off toward Wolly.

G.I. chuckled as he left out of the store.

"It's nice to see you converse with a guy without killing him," Wolly teased.

"Oh, don't get it twisted. He was about thirty seconds away from being maggot food," Assata asserted, even though her body language displayed something different.

"You lie to me. I can see very good. You like him," exclaimed Wolly in his heavy Arabian accent.

Assata blushed, causing her dimple to form deeply. "He a'ight," she downplayed. "On some other shit, though, Wolly, I wanted to come in here and thank you. The footage you gave them for my case really saved me. I owe you my loyalty foreva! Whateva you need me to handle, just say it. I'm on top of that shit."

"Don't worry about that. You owe me nothing. As a matter of fact, here." Wolly handed Assata a set of keys.

"What's this?" She was perplexed.

"The apartment upstairs. It was your grandfather's, then your father's. Now, it's yours."

Assata looked at the keys then back at Wolly. "Are you serious?"

"Yes! Don't be weird, take it." Wolly started waving his hand dismissively.

"Thank you, man."

"No problem. I cleaned it a little, but mainly left it the way your father did. And, don't worry about rent. Another thing, I wanted to ask you: How do you get currency?"

"Whateva, however! Why wassup?"

"I left something in the room for you. If you like, you keep. If not, I'll take care of it."

"Okay, I'm headed up there now. I'ma letchu know wassup."

"Okay."

Assata made her way out of the store and was confounded to find G.I. leaning on Ketta's Benz with pizzazz. She found his antics disrespectfully amusing.

"Leaning on stranger's property, huh? I see you don't mind dying," Assata pronounced, swiftly pulling a pocket rocket from her Moschino hoodie.

"We been properly introduced, so we're no longer strangers," G.I asserted, approaching Assata. While her hand was on the trigger, G.I. grabbed the barrel and placed it in the middle of his forehead. "Some shit in life worth dying for," he said, philosophizing.

Assata's pussy throbbed and became soaked as she shifted uncomfortably.

Damn, every time this nigga talk, it feels like he kissing on my flesh and shit, Assata thought.

"Boy you is crazy!"

"How 'bout you let me be that."

"Be what?"

"Crazy bout'chu," G.I. replied, showing two rows of glistening white teeth in an infectious smile.

Assata's mouth hung open, caught up in his vernacular stare. G.I. removed the pistol from his forehead and snuck a kiss in, sucking on Assata's top lip.

Damn, this nigga lips soft! thought Assata.

"Um-Ummm! Boy, don't put yo' fuckin' lips on me!" Assata pulled away from his grasp and headed behind the store to check out the apartment.

"Let me get'cha number, ma."

"Not today!"

"I'ma get'chu!"

"Whateva!" Assata made her way up the stairs feeling conflicted. Even thought she was a virgin, her and her pussy knew that G.I. could get it.

***

Assata entered the apartment and noted the decor being Versace everything. She was displeased to see that there were no photos of any kind, anywhere of her grandfather or father. Moving through the living room which shared the same space as the kitchen, Assata headed to the room in the back of the apartment.

"Damn, this shit laid, on some real bachelor type shit," Assata muttered as she headed to the window and peered through the designer drapes. She saw that everything could be seen from her viewpoint. "Nice," she thought out loud. When she turned around, she gazed at what Wolly had gifted her with. Twenty pounds of Train Wreck in vacuum sealed bags, and twenty-thousand dollars in all blue faces. After taking it all in, Assata headed downstairs to tell Wolly thank you, and that she accepted his offer.

Chapter 6
AINT 'CHU A KILLA?

"Sss...ooh, daddy, ffffuck. Yeah!" Lee Lee moaned, gripping the handle of Hassan's wheelchair bouncing chaotically on his dick. Both her legs stretched over the arms of the wheelchair. Hassan palmed both of her succulent ass cheeks.

"Ffffuck! Ssss... Damn! Um in that pussy!" Hassan cried as his eyes rolled to the back of his head.

"Yes, daddy, you deep! Sss... oooh, you deep in this pussy!" Lee Lee groaned through clenched teeth.

"Ol' shittt! Sss... shit, um finna, skee, sss...FFFuck!" Hassan felt his nut conjure up from his toes, to up his spine and out of his shaft.

Timing his climax perfectly, Lee Lee hopped off his dick and caught his nut with her mouth. She moaned while sucking the soul from Hassan's body.

"Oh my Gawd!" Hassan cried, shaking like a '57 Chevy with no plug. Lee Lee continued to suck the head of his dick until it tickled. "Ssshit! That's enough." Hassan stated pushing Lee Lee's head away from his dick.

Lee Lee laughed and stood to her feet. "You can't handle this good pussy and head?"

"Bitch, I'm paraplegic. You don't get no points for that." Hassan retorted, catching his breath.

"It's, okay. Baby, you still my daddy." LeeLee leaned in to kiss Hassan, but he turned his head. "Oh, you can't kiss me after sucking yo' dick? Nigga, it's yo' dick!"

"Ion suck dick; you do! Miss a nigga wit' all that extra shit."

"Get somebody else to suck ya dick then, nigga," Lee Lee stated putting her clothes back on.

"Yeah, whatever. Listen, though. I gotta holla at'chu 'bout some real shit."

"What, Hassan?" Lee Lee was apparently upset with him.

"Look. Some niggas put some money on my head for killin' them people. Some kinda way, they know you was wit' me on them plays."

Lee Lee showed no distress. "And?"

"I got a few dollars put up. I want you to take it and go to another state. I'll meet up wit'chu later, after I take care of that bidness."

"Nigga, you got me fucked up! I ain't going nowhere! They kill you, they might as well push my shit back, too."

"Lee Lee, please, man! Please just go! For me, bae, please!" Hassan begged.

"Ain't you a killa?"

"You know how I'm comin'."

"Well kill them niggas, 'cause I ain't goin' nowhere! My sister Tasha still ain't popped up yet. I'm not goin' no fuckin' where!"

Hassan exhaled in defeat. It would hurt him deeply if Lee Lee forced him to kill her. His love for her was paramount.

Before he could continue to play with Lee Lee, Assata sauntered in the room with casual arrogance. She noted that Hassan appeared to be stewing with frustration. "You good, bra?"

"Yeah, I'm good, lil' sis."

"You sho?" Assata took a seat in a custom-made Laz-E Boy that belonged to Patty's husband D-Dog.

"I said I'm good."

"A'ight then. Lee Lee, wassup? You a'ight?" Assata implored with a devilish grin.

"Yeah, girl. I'm good."

"I'm just checkin' 'cause the last phone call we had, you sounded a lil' tight."

Hassan gave Assata an evaluative look.

"I was just vexed 'bout my people. Girl, you know we are good. You my sis-in-law." Lee Lee laughed.

"I hear you," Assata retorted contemplatively.

"Shit, fie that dope up." Lee Lee stated referred to the blunt Assata had between her fingers.

"Hey, yeah, fire that shit up," Hassan added, snagging the blunt from Assata. He attempted to put it between his lips, but Lee Lee snatched it and put flame to it. She took five pulls and inhaled deeply. "Damn, Queen Hoover!" Clowned Hassan.

Moments later Lee Lee's eyes grew wide as she fell face first on the fluffy carpet.

"Bae!" cried Hassan. Lee Lee laid in an awkward position, paralyzed.

Assata squatted and rolled her over. "Sis-n-law, are you a'ight ?"

Lee Lee began to shake and foam at the mouth.

"Assata, help her," Hassan begged.

"For what, nigga?" Assata replied through clenched teeth.

Hassan knew Assata was responsible for Lee Lee's condition. "What the fuck did you do?" Hassan cried, running his hands through his locks.

"I just laced the blunt with poisons— Thallium salt and a lil' fent-fent," Assata admitted, smiling demon-like.

"You was gone let me fie that blunt up?"

"Shid, the way you were trying to convince her to take yo' lil' money and leave town, I figured you chose sides. So, hell yeah, I was gon' let'chu."

Hassan shook his head as he watched Lee Lee take her last breath. Blood and vomit puddled around her head. "I loved that hoe, sis. I couldn't just kill her like that. She was there for me."

"Nigga, fuck all that! When you was in a coma, I was the one out there putting the murder game down! Me!" Assata banged her fist against her chest.

"And, I love you for that, lil' sis, but damn." Hassan shook his head.

Assata gazed at her brother in disgust. "Nigga, it's family over everything, but'chu actin' like you live by a different creed."

Hassan rubbed his hand over his face contemplating Assata's words. "You right, sis. I love you, and I apologize. We all we got."

Assata stood, hugged Hassan neck, and kissed him on the forehead. "I forgive you for now."

"So, what's next?"

"After I put this hoe in the creek, we gon' shop for our new house."

Chapter 7
WATCH MY SIX

Two Weeks Later...

Assata and Hassan were in the living room of their new home, relaxed on a peanut butter colored sectional. They took shots of 1800 Tequila Reposado while Assata painted a picture of how she ran down on the niggaz who shot Hassan. While detailing how the bodies were dropping.

Assata's phone rang. "Hello?"

"Assata, wassup? Are you busy?" asked Ketta.

"Wassup, ma? Not really. Me and Hassan just politicking. Why? Wassup?"

"I need you to ride wit' me somewhere, if you don't mind."

"Okay. Where at?"

"Come outside."

"I'll be out there." Assata hung up and turned to Hassan. "Ketta wants me to step out wit' her for a few. You gon' be aight?" she asked, standing and stretching.

"Yah, I'm good. I'ma just blow Loud and watch this BMF series," retorted Hassan.

"Aight. Hit me if you need me." Assata kissed Hassan on the forehead and headed outside.

Ketta sat behind the tint of her unmarked Infiniti truck as Assata appeared and hopped in the passenger seat.

"Wassup, ma?" Assata greeted, kissing Ketta on the cheek.

"Hey, baby girl. How you feelin'?"

"I'm, just vibin'."

"As you should. Listen. You wit' me?"

"You know this! Whateva, however! Come on, man, act like you know," Assata stated significantly.

"You don't even know what I'm speakin' on."

"Whatever, however!" Declared Assata.

"That's my baby girl! Let's roll." Ketta backed out of the driveway and headed to their destination. "Jump in the backseat and put all that on," Ketta instructed.

When Assata jumped in the back seat, she noted a pair of all black cargo jeans, a black long sleeve t-shirt, a vest that read *FEDS* on it, a pair of black boots, and a mini AR-15.

"Some gangsta shit, huh? Okay then, ma." Assata smiled with satisfaction. "When it get gaaanngsta!" Assata quoted a line from a Texas rapper named Z-Ro.

"I told you, I'ma sho' you how I get down." Ketta pronounced. Eight minutes later, she backed into a parking lot made out of dirt that sat in front of a park off of Oleander.

"What the play is, ma?" Assata implored, strapping on the vest and grabbing the AR-15.

"Okay, look. I got these Bahamian motherfuckers I been investigating for six months. My colleague wants to hit 'em next week, but we're going to hit em' tonight. Just follow my lead, baby girl, and watch my six."

"I gotcha, ma."

"You know how to work that AR?"

Assata chambered a round, then gave Ketta an assuring look.

"Okay, we lit." Ketta strapped her vest on then grabbed a modified Glock 17 equipped with a green beam. Moments later, a Dodge Hornet pulled into a beautiful home that sat across the street from the park. Ketta pulled behind the target aggressively and hopped out with Assata following her lead.

The Bahamian stepped out of his vehicle with his hand blocking the light from Ketta's Glock.

"*Federal Agents! Get the fuck on the ground! Lay the fuck down, right na!*" Ketta order.

"Okay! Don't shoot! I'm unarmed! Please, don't shoot!" the victim pleaded, laying on the ground. Assata stood over him while Ketta placed the cuffs on.

"Who else in the house?" asked Ketta.

"Nobody," the Bahamian was visibly shaken.

"You Amos, right?" Ketta questioned, removing the key he had clutched in his hand.

"Yeah."

"Okay, get up. We going inside." Ketta helped Amos to his feet and took him to the front door. "Which key is it?"

"The yellow one."

Ketta opened the door and pushed Amos into the house and onto the floor. Assata followed, closing the door behind her.

"Why, you only two here? You imposter!" Amos proclaimed in his heavy Bahamian accent. Assata moved in and hit Amos in the bridge of his nose, breaking it instantly. He moaned in agony.

"I'm only gonna ask you once. Where it at?" Ketta gritted.

"Don't know what you mean."

Ketta grabbed him by his mini-afro and jammed her Glock in his mouth. "Where the fuck that work at, nigga!" Ketta snarled through clenched teeth, then snatched the Glock out of his mouth.

"Backyard in the *tingom!*"

Assata went to search the rest of the house.

"Baby girl, hold up." Ketta stopped Assata. "What the fuck is a *tingom?*"

"Backyard, in da boat," answered Amos.

"Hold him down 'til I get back," Ketta ordered then headed out back.

"Where the fuck is the money at?" Asked Assata.

Amos spat the blood from his mouth, caused by Ketta's Glock.

"Inside the closet, on the floor. Move the rug; you'll see it."

"What closet?"

"Behind you." Assata turned and headed towards the closet when someone appeared out of the hallway. Out of pure instinct, Assata let it rip from the AR, dropping and killing its target instantly. Approaching and standing over the body. Assata saw that it was a little girl. It was Amos' twelve-year-old daughter. "Damn," muttered Assata. She was conflicted as she maneuvered through the rest of the house to make sure it was clear.

Amos could be heard wailing from the death of his daughter. After clearing the house, Assata made her way back to the closet and retrieved the money.

"Baby girl!" Ketta called from the living room.

When Assata sped out of the closet, she had a vacuum sealed bag containing $150,000, and noted that Ketta had a bag in her hand.

"My daughter!" cried Amos hoarsely.

"Baby girl, what the fuck?"

"She came outta nowhere. I took her down," Assata explained, stepping over the body.

"Fuck!"

"I tried to clear the house, but'chu stopped me. She startled me, and you looking at the outcome," Assata replied impassively.

Ketta exhaled. "We gotta go." Ketta stood over Amos while he gazed at his daughter's lifeless body, and planted two on the side of his head. The duo then left the home and jumped into the truck Ketta backed out and left the scene unnoticed. "I should've let'chu clear the house, that's on me. A lot of heat gon' come behind that lil' girl, but it is what it is. We gon' break down and lay low." Ketta glanced at Assata, attempting to read her mind. "Baby girl, you good?"

Assata used her right hand to flip her dreads to the back of her head. "Yeah, ma, I'm aight."

"Okay. Thank you for coming wit' me. I love you."

"Love you, too," Assata replied just above a whisper.

Chapter 8
DEMON-TIME

After the Bahamian and his daughter were discovered, the city was crawling with cops. The double homicide even brought the First 48 into town. When Ketta felt like things were cooler, she gave Assata two bricks of coke, $50,000 and the keys to her Benz. She used the apartment that Wolly gave her to stash everything else. Leaving her apartment, she was surprised to see G.I. leaning on her car once again. Drippin' in confidence and suavity, Assata was smitten by his presence but tried to disguise it.

"Wassup, Dimples? You missed me?" G.I. asked with his arms folded across his chest.

Assata's eyes navigated from his muscular arms down to the print that was shaped beneath his Billionaire Boys Club sweats.

G.I. used his index finger to lift Assata's chin and overt her attention back to him. "Don't let'cha eyes overload ya lust."

Assata slapped his hand away. "Nigga, you outta pocket!"

"Am I?"

"Hell yeah! Seems to me you a whole stalker out'chea," Assata pronounced with her hands on her hips.

"It's all about perspective, ma."

"Meaning?"

"Any outside party who know no better may find my antics to be enigmatic, or a bit stalkerish. On the contrary, every fiber of your being is telling me that you find my actions brazen and charming." G.I. closed the space between them and placed a tender kiss on Assata's succulent lips.

Assata reciprocated and moaned as the typhoon stirred between her legs. G.I.'s hands traveled down the deep arch of Assata's back, finding their way to her cotton soft posterior, grabbing both cheeks firmly. The stimulation between her legs became too overwhelming, causing Assata to break away from G.I.'s grasp. "What the fuck do you want from me, man?" Assata impulsively shouted.

"Everything," G.I. replied calmly.

"You don't even know me!"

"Well, let me learn you."

Assata gazed at the moving traffic, then back into G.I.'s titillating eyes, and exhaled deeply. "I'm not who you think I am. Don't let this outside appearance fool you. I'm on straight demon time."

"I'on mind exorcising them demons," G.I. countered smoothly. Assata's smile was irrepressible. He shook his head and chuckled.

"Boy, you too much for yo' damn self," Assata pronounced.

G.I. pulled Assata closer and kissed her on both of her dimples. Assata obliged and kissed him back passionately as if they'd known each other in another lifetime.

G.I. drew away from the kiss. "So tell me, what'chu got planned this evening?"

****

The moonlight danced on top of the water as the currents moved swiftly at a beach known as "The River", creating the perfect setting. Assata leaned against her car door and enjoyed the vibe that G.I. was given her.

"So, what side of town you from?" questioned Assata.

"All over. I lived on every side of the city."

"Why so?"

G.I. rubbed his hands over his face, not really wanting to discuss the reason. "I was a troubled youngin. My mother died when I was five, leaving me wit' my lil' sister and father. Me and my pops bumped heads a lot so I stayed in the streets until I found my way."

"If you don't mind me askin', what happened to your mom, and where is your sister and your dad now?"

"I'll tell you some other time. Not right na, ma," pronounced G.I. moving closer to Assata.

"Okay. I respect that. So, why they call you G.I.?"

"God's Image."

Assata smiled and nodded in approval. "That's cute."

"Plus, I be *goin' in*," he added.

"Goin' in on what?"

"Everything!" G.I. moved in and kissed Assata on her forehead, nose, and lips.

While kissing her tenderly, his hands stroked her neck softly, causing Assata to gasp in the sudden sensual act. Still a virgin, Assata felt a confused mixture of fear and longing. Fear rose as her eyes raced across the landscape while contemplating her predicament. It was dark and deserted, with no one anywhere in view. G.I. removed his hands from Assata's neck, and turned her around. He then placed her hands on the top of the car. He knelt and began to stroke Assata's bare calves. She fought to hold on to her fear that was dissolving into her heart's desire. His hands moved slowly up Assata's legs, squeezing and stroking along the way.

"You can tell me to stop at any time," voiced G.I. as he inhaled.

Assata remained silent. G.I. gripped the hem of her tight fitted skirt, and lifted it as he continued making his way to her thighs, exposing her meaty, smooth ass cheeks to him and the night sky. Hiking the skirt around Assata's waist, G.I. squeezed and smacked Assata's ass, smirking as she groaned. He reached between her legs, fingering the creamy wetness now staining her laced panties. He slapped her ass harder, prompting Assata to gasp and arch her back.

"You want me?" G.I. whispered.

Assata remained mute, but breathed heavily.

Smack! G.I. slapped her right cheek harder. "Answer me!" he demanded in a seductive growl as he pulled Assata's panties down, forcing her to stumble. G.I. lifted one of her feet, leaving the laced panties around the other ankle. He parted her cheeks and slipped his tongue inside her asshole, forcing Assata to lift up and scratch the roof of the car.

"Oooh...fffuck!" cried Assata. "Please, don't stop." Assata growled through clenched teeth.

G.I. removed his tongue, eased his thumb into her ass then slipped a finger inside her pulsing, tight pussy.

Calling on her Creator, Assata struggled to keep her knees locked as G.I. worked magic with his hands. Assata threw her pussy backwards, tightening her inner muscles while trying to push G.I. deeper. But he withdrew his fingers.

"Tell me to stop," the bass in G.I.'s voice was an aphrodisiac.

Assata shook her head, throwing her dreads about in a manner that G.I. found attractive. His hands slid along Assata's trembling inner thighs. He pushed a finger back into her dripping pussy and pumped her slowly while his other hand massaged her ass.

"You want me to fuck you?" G.I. teased, pushing a second and then a third finger inside Assata's pussy. Assata moaned in pure bliss. "Answer me! You want this dick inside you?" he asked aggressively.

An orgasm was rising in Assata. "Please, don't stop," she begged. "Yes…Yes! I want'chu to fuck me!" she screamed on the verge of climaxing. She threw her pussy back to G.I.'s rhythm, her insides clenching and unclenching spasmodically. G.I. suddenly smacked Assata's ass hard.

"Sss…OOoh ffuck!" moaned Assata.

G.I. smacked her ass again harder, all the while he continued a slow manipulation of Assata's insides. "You don't nut until I tell you to! "You hear me?"

Smack! G.I. slapped her ass again hard. His hands were coated and dripping with her cream. He began pumping his fingers harder and deeper in her pussy, while spanking one cheek then the other. Assata's body buckled but G.I. kept her pinned against the car. He pulled his hand almost out of her, then slammed it back in.

"FFFucck! Please...Please...Just fuck me," Assata chanted.

"Shut the fuck up! You get fucked when I say so!" *Smack! Smack!* "You can cum now!" *Smack!*

Moments later, she cried in sweet bliss as her knees buckled. G.I. held his hand deep inside her as Assata's hot pussy pulsed around it.

"That's a good girl," G.I. said withdrawing his fingers and sucking them clean.

"Ssss...Oooww," Assata cried while attempting to stop her body from quivering.

G.I. cupped the source of Assata's heat in his palm until the throbbing stopped. He stood and turned Assata to him, smirking slightly as he watched her struggle to gain some measure of composure. All toughness and demon-time that Assata claimed to be on was gone. She appeared to be bewildered. Her eyes were soft, her lips were wet and parted slightly. As she pulled in a small gasp of breath, G.I. knelt in the soft sand and leveled his face with Assata's pretty pussy. His mouth watered at her hardened clit that sat perfectly between her plump outer lips. Assata placed her hand on G.I.'s dreads, her fingers digging into his scalp as he led his mouth to her throbbing pussy. G.I. licked and sucked, moving to Assata's rhythm.

"Oh...Shhh...ssshhit!" Assata screamed through clenched teeth.

He felt Assata's body tense, her clit pulsing on his tongue. She pressed his face hard on her pussy and held it there. He moaned at the taste of Assata's cream as she came. Feeling the intensity of Assata's release, G.I.'s body responded in kind, releasing pre-cum beneath his Armani Exchange briefs and on his thighs. After devouring all of Assata's juices, G.I. stood and kissed her deeply.

"I love how you taste," G.I. mentioned above a whisper.

"I love how you taste, it," Assata replied, still galvanized from the orgasm.

G.I. knelt again and pulled Assata's panties from around her ankle. He knocked the sand from them and handed them to her.

"You ain't gon' give me the dick?"

"Not tonight, dimples," G.I. replied smiling.

"This nigga here," Assata pronounced, shaking her head in disbelief. "What type of time you on, man?"

"Demon time!" G.I. retorted smirking.

Chapter 9
PRETTY LADY

The parking lot was crowded and busy when Ketta pulled into the Wal-Mart Supercenter in Port St. Lucie. After making her way around the parking lot, she parked next to Charity's Mercedes Benz AMG S63, and moments later Charity exited her vehicle then hopped into Ketta's. Charity was the Forensic Lab Technician who ran the DNA on Khafre's red rag. After doing Ketta a solid, Charity called and asked Ketta to return the favor.

"How you doing tonight, sexy?" Charity greeted flirtatiously.

"I'm good, how are you?" Ketta responded.

"Well, since I'm in the presence of you, I'm cool," Charity exclaimed, licking her lips.

Ketta watched her intensely. She found Charity to be a royal beauty, just not beautiful enough to make her switch teams. Charity sported a low-cut hairstyle and resembled the singer Muni Long. She was a slim, thick beauty.

"I'm honored to make your day. Na, we get to the bidness."

"All work, no play, huh?"

"It's the only thing that makes sense to me. Na, run me my money."

Charity pulled the left side on her bra down, exposing her beautiful B-Cup size breast. She grabbed a wad of money that fell from her bra and handed it to Ketta. "Oops," Charity stated sarcastically.

Ketta shook her head and smiled. "Bitch, you crazy," Ketta pruned counting the money. It was $1,200. "Look under the seat."

Charity reached under the seat and pulled out a brown paper bag. "Damn! I smell this shit through the bag." Charity pulled the ounce from the bag. "Oow! I ain't even hit this yet and I got the bubble guts. This is that butter!"

"Okay, I got shit to handle. Pleasure doin' bidness wit'chu," said Ketta.

"Wait, hold up. How much of this shit can you get?" asked Charity putting the dope back in the bag.

"Whatever you got, I'ma make it happen."

"Okay, well, look. I am hitting these parties. It's a bunch of rich white folks, and they be running through a lot of dope. "You can make a killin!"

"I'on know 'bout all that," Ketta replied contemplatively.

"Just come to one party." Begged Charity. "I'll just give you the work and let'chu make the play. Just bring me my cut."

"You know I work a lot! I'm not gonna be able to move when they call all the time. I'm tryna put'chu on some real money, and you actin' flake!"

Ketta thought about it for a moment. "How much do they pay for a zip?"

"It's a bunch of white folk wit' money! Bitch, you put'cha own price on it."

Ketta gazed out of her window for a moment then back at Charity. "When's the next party?"

***

When Ketta and Charity arrived at the party the driveway of the mansion was filled with a mixture of Ford 650 mud trucks with lift kits, Benz, and BMWs.

"Bitch, you see how nice this place is?" Charity questioned, smiling from ear to ear.

"Yeah, I see it. I see that racist ass rebel flag, too," countered Ketta.

"Girl, these mothafuckers ain't racist. They just patriotic."

"You sho you know the difference between the two?"

"Ketta, you trippin'. Bitch, come get this money. Fuck the bullshit."

"Let me ask you something. What the fuck do you get outta this?"

"A few thousand and a wet pussy. Heeyyy!" Charity boasted, licking her tongue out.

Ketta exhaled deeply then grabbed her Chanel clutch. "Let's just get this over with." She stepped out in a pair of black-heeled velvet pumps that laced up to her knees and a tight fitted vintage Chanel Haute courier dress. Her wavy hair was pulled back into a French bun while her edges were perfectly slid across the front and side of her face.

Charity stepped out in a Balenciaga bodysuit and heels with a Gucci clutch. "Damn, that ass sitting right in that dress," Charity complimented Ketta.

Ketta shook her head when she realized how tight Charity's body suit was. "So, you just gon' waltz in here in front of all those white folk wit' all that pussy sittin' in front of you like that?"

"This what they like, girl," Charity informed, petting her meaty pussy.

"Tsss...! Just lead the way so we can get this shit over with." Ketta was a little annoyed. She could hear country music coming from inside.

"Ugggh...! Grumpy are we?" said Charity as she walked off seductively up the cobble-stoned driveway that led to an electronic gate. Charity pressed the button and waited. "Come on, girl," Charity told Ketta who was walking a little slowly .

"State your business," the voice from the intercom ordered.

"Party, Party, Party!" Charity retorted excitedly.

"Password?"

"Cocaine!" answered Charity.

Moments later, the gate opened. Charity grabbed Ketta's hand and led her to the ten-foot redwood doors.

Ketta noted the columns in the front of the massive home. "This some real plantation architecture type shit."

"Well, we finna get some of this plantation type money," Charity proclaimed. The front doors opened and a red neck that resembled Kid Rock stepped out in a cowboy hat, flannel long sleeve shirt, Wranglers and some cowboy boots. "Howdy!" Greeted Bob as he hugged Charity.

"Heyy, big daddy, how have you been? You missed me?" Charity asked while hugging Bob's waist.

"Like a Seminole misses swamp cabbage."

Ketta's face crumpled in disgust.

"Awwl, I miss you, daddy. This is my friend, Ketta. Ketta, this is Bob."

At that moment, Ketta wished that she had given Charity a fake name for the party.

"Howdy!" Bob lifted his hat as a respectable gesture, placed it back on his head, and attempted to hug Ketta.

She placed her hand on his chest and pushed him back a step. "Social distancing, cowboy."

"Covid's over, darling," Bob said in a strong southern accent.

"You believe that?"

"Well, aren't you adorable?" Bob smiled, grabbed a water bottle from his back pocket, and spit into it.

Ketta despised people who dipped.

"Come on in, and welcome to Cocaine Mansion." Bob invited the women inside.

When Ketta stepped inside she noticed the custom chandeliers and curving staircase in the foyer. The flooring had a venetian marble style when she ventured further into the spacious living area that had towering ceilings. A gang of people could be seen sitting around a Gyrofocus 360-degrees rotating fireplace that hung from the ceiling. Out in the open, everyone could clearly be seen snorting cocaine. Ketta recognized a few of them from her line of work. Judge Nelson, a lawyer named Michael Ole, and a few detectives. She even saw her partner Peter. Bob pulled Ketta into the kitchen.

"You holding? Charity told me that you got that good shit." When Ketta turned to look for Charity, she was nowhere in sight.

"Yeah, what'chu need?"

"You gotta ounce on you?"

"Yeah, three-thousand."

"Well, that's fine with me, pretty lady," Bob assured, pulling out his wallet and counting out three-thousand. Ketta took the money, then pulled an ounce from her clutch.

"Pleasure doing business with you, darling. You just feel free to make yourself at home." Bob lifted his hat then disappeared.

"Damn, three-thousand for an ounce?" Ketta said to herself. After stuffing the money in her clutch, Ketta peeked around a corner wall, and saw the governor of Florida with an underage girl in his lap. Ketta quickly removed her phone to get a few pictures. As soon as she focused on him and everyone around him in the picture, Judge Nelson lowered her head to snort a line of coke. Ketta took the picture with perfect timing.

"Got'chu bitch," Ketta pronounced smirking devilishly. She headed back into the kitchen and slipped into a spacious halfway that was connected to it, And heard the sounds of a woman being pleasured.

"Sss… Aahh!! Yess, daddy right there! Sss… Whoooo… Ssshit" Curious, Ketta grabbed the door handle, opened it, and peeped inside.

"That's it, Ssss....ohhh. I'm finna skeet on that tongue!"
Ketta was astounded to find her partner, Peter eating
Charity's pussy.

"This shit wild," Ketta whispered, grabbing her phone.
Charity was sitting on top of a red wood dresser rolling and
winding her puss in Peter's face, when she took the picture.
Ketta closed the door and continued down the hallway that
led to a panorama of many acres. Gazing out of the massive
windows, Ketta spotted another familiar face.

"I know that aint...This shit can't get no stranger,"
muttered Ketta, snapping multiple photos. After putting her
phone away, she made a left turn that led to the main level
family room. The room was packed with all sorts of officials
performing degenerate, and dotish acts. Ketta slipped past
them and out of a massive door that led to an outside kitchen,
pool and spa surrounded by palms, tropical foliage, and
cascading water features. Ketta approached the familiar face,
who was sitting comfortably on a sofa with his head laid
back, receiving fellatio from an underage girl. Ketta cleared
her throat. The familiar man lifted his head, exposing a nose
full of cocaine. Ketta's presence didn't stop the young girl
from performing her duty.

"Ken Mascura," Ketta greeted.

"Ketta," Mascura replied, sniffing and wiping coke
residue from his nose and thick mustache.

Ken Mascura was the head sheriff for the city of Fort
Pierce. He had his hands in some of everything.

"How the fuck you know my name?" Ketta asked,
shifting uncomfortably.

"It's my got dam town," he retorted with a satanic smirk.
"Anybody, that's making any noise, from the small street
punks, to the kingpin... I know about 'em."

"You don't know shit about me."

"The hell if I don't," Ken countered impassively.

"Okay, look! Tell this lil bitch, to excuse herself."

"What in the hell for? She ain't bothering you none," Mascura pronounced with a redneck drawl. Ketta grabbed the young redhead by her hair and snatched her up.

"Go, find you some Fisher Price shit to play with" insisted Ketta.

"Na, why'd you go do that for? You just ruined a good nut! I was almost finish, gotdamit!"

"Fuck all that! How do you know me?" inquired Ketta. Mascura grabbed a spaghetti bowl of yay off of a dark green granite table and stuck his face inside it. He snorted intensely then sat the bowl back down.

"I know you, detective. You're dating that Khafre fella who killed them federal agents," Ken proclaimed tucking his small pecker back in his tight wranglers.

"I don't know what'chu talkin bout," lied Ketta.

"The hell you don't. Just like I reckon, you don't know who killed that Bahamian and his daughter."

Ketta's heart rate increased, but soon after relaxed when she realized she had a photo of him getting his dick sucked by a minor.

"You fuckin right! I'on know shit about shit!" she announced, voice thickening with menace. Unfazed by Ketta's tone, he stuck his nose in the bowl again. He then sat back grinning with ill-surprised-satisfaction before speaking again.

"This is how this is going, moving forward. I set'em up, you knock'em down.. 50-50 split! You work for me now!"

"And if I refuse?"

"Is that a rhetorical question?" Ken asked sardonically.

Ketta exhaled and shook her head. "I'll play yo lil game for now," Ketta declared standing to leave.

"Charity said that you'd have something for me."

She turned and looked at Ken in disbelief. "Look like you don't need shit else to me."

"Come on with it, pretty lady" Ken retorted, motioning his hand for her to hand it over.

"Three-thousand!" Ketta spat.

Ken laughed before replying. "Gotta have my 50 percent."

Ketta reached in her clutch, threw an ounce at him and walked away.

"See you soon, pretty lady."

Chapter 10
I KNOW A KILLA WHEN I SEE ONE

It was a hot, but beautiful day on Avenue S. Hassan had been up hustling and smoking blunts back to back since 6 a.m. Thoughts of his brother Husain, his father, and Lee Lee have been invaded his mind lately, enabling him to receive the proper sleep. He sat in his electric wheelchair, pistol in lap, inside the garage with the glass sliding doors open, smoking when a 2021 Mercedes- Benz GIS 600 Maybach pulled into his driveway. It was painted a custom black, sitting on 22 inch factory rims. Hassan clutched his pistol as a young'n hopped out the driver's side and approached.

"Wass popping, OG?"

"Who the fuck is you, lil nigga!" Hassan asked, still clutching his pistol observing what the youngin had on. He was dipped in an all-black Dickie suit, with a pair of Nike Kobe 5 'Undefeated Hall of Fame' Edition.

"Dey call me, Lil Fif God."

"Okay. Da fuck, you doing in my driveway?"

Lil Fif raised his hands on the air. "I ain't on nothing OG. I'm just looking for something to smoke."

"What make you think this where it's at?"

"A lil hoe I'm fucking pointed me in this direction. Look OG, if you don't want to serve me. I'll just rotate somewhere else," Lil Fif started heading back to the truck.

"Wait, hold up, lil homie." Lil Fif stopped to see what Hassan had to say. "What'chu looking for?"

Lil Fif approached again. "I just wanna 8th, my nigga."

Hassan shook his head up and down. "I got'chu. Who that, in the truck wit'cha?' Hassan nodded towards the truck.

"Thats my nigga, Shooter. He solid." Lil Fif assured.

"I hear you. Nice truck. What'chu lil niggaz into?"

"We just some, lil all around street niggas. We get it how we get it. Shid.. I ain't gone kapp. That ain't my truck. A cracka left this mothafucka runnin' at the gas station. We just took it."

"How old you is?"

"I'm fifteen. My nigga fifteen too."

"Where y'all from?"

"S.L.G."s

"Sunland Garden, huh? Tell 'em get out," Hassan instructed. Lil Fif God motioned for Shooter to get out of the truck. Shooter hopped out of the Benz truck also dipped in an all-black Dickie suit in a pair of Nike Dunk Low X off-white 'The 50' Collection. He was a dark skinned youngsta that sported a high top fade. Just off first glance, Hassan could tell why his name was Shooter. His eyes depicted a villainous soul. Lil Fif God was light skinned with a low 9-5 cut. He had deep waves and tattoo's on his face down to his legs. Lil Fif seemed more reserved but sneakily if need be.

"Wassup, lil homie?"

"What up with it?" Shooter retorted.

"Your homie, Lil Fif was just speaking highly of you. I thought it was only right to meet'cha. I'm Hassan."

"Shooter," Shooter replied, dapping Hassan up the way that gangstas do.

"Look here, man," Hassan said, reaching in his brief and pulling out an ounce. "Y'all take this shit here." Lil Fif grabbed the ounce from Hassan.

"How much, OG?" Questioned Lil Fif.

"That's on me. Y'all lil niggaz, smoke out."

"Damn OG. That's some real shit."

"Hell yeah!" Shooter said, grabbing the ounce from Lil Fif and smelling it.

"I think I got some shit you might want OG," Fif proclaimed walking to the truck and returning with a duffle bag. He sat the bag down in front of Hassan and unzipped it. The bag was full of prescription pills and bottles of Codeine.

"Damn! How the fuck you run across this shit?"

"We hit a pharmacy," answered Lil Fif.

"Whatchu want for this?"

"Just give us two-bands a piece," Shooter assorted.

"I call that."

***

Two weeks later…

Assata pulled into the driveway on Avenue S with G.I, in the passenger seat of the new Tahoe supercharged Yenko truck. It was all white, black 22 inch factory rims with black interior. When Assata told G.I. what she had going on, he helped her move both keys and ten pounds of the loud with no pressure. Intrigued by his actions, Assata grew fond of him. G.I. had yet to penetrate her, but still threw rocks at the chain gang to help her put food on the table. For the life of Assata, she couldn't understand it, but she loved it. Assata noticed a crowd of white people leaving out of her garage and hopping into their vehicles that were parked all over the place.

"Da fuck?"

"What's good, Dimples?" asked G.I. concerned.

"Who the fuck all deez white folks in my shit? Wait out here for me." Assata stated grabbing a black trash bag from the backseat and hopping out.

"Who the fuck is y'all?" Assata asked a young pimpled faced redhead with braces in her mouth.

"I was just here to see the San Man," the redhead replied and scurried to her vehicle. Assata made her way through the glass sliding doors, and into garage. Weed smoke fogged the entire garage, and bottles of Patron and Codeine were all over a coffee table that sat in the middle of the garage.

"Who the fuck, dem Krakaz was leaving out my shit?"! Assata questions.

"Hold up, sis, "Hassan replied, his words slightly slowed due to the codeine.

"This…My….Shit….Too. This…Our..Shit. and them Krackkas….came to…seee me. The san man."Assata tried hard not to laugh at Hassan.

"The San Man?"

"Yeaahh! Thats..my…dope boy..name..San Man. You..got it…sis…right? Hassan..The Sand Man. Huh? You get it?"

Assata couldn't hold it any longer. She laughed at how foolish Hassan was acting, but was glad that he was enjoying himself. "So what do they come to see you for?"

Hassan nodded his head towards a duffle bag that sat next to his wheelchair. Assata placed her trash bag next to the duffle, then unzipped the duffle bag and seen all the prescriptions and bottles of codeine.

"Where you get all this shit from?" Hassan nodded his head to the other side of the garage. With no heartbeat of hesitation, Assata drew her baby pocket rocket FN.25 from her Burlington sweats and aimed it at two figures that was sitting in thc cut of hcr garage.

"Chiiiilll…Sis…They…wit' me," Hassan informed.

Lil Fif God rose in from of the crevice of the garage and approached Assata who still had the pistol aimed at him.

"Calm down, beautiful. Won't chu gone put that lil thing away before you hurt somebody," Lil Fif stated in a calm and smooth tone.

"Yeah, we can't afford to have any mishaps in here, ya heard me," Shooter added also approached Assata.

Lil Fif God extended his hand for Assata to shake it. "They call me, Lil Fif God. It's nice to finally meet'chu." Assata tucked her pistol away and shook Lil Fif's hand.

"Wassup boss lady, they call me shooter."

"What dey do?"Assata retrored shaking his hand.

"Deez my..Lil niggaz....Sis." Hassan added.

"Okay then. So, why they call you? Lil Fif God?" questioned Assata, impressed with how both youngins carried themselves thus far.

"Kuz I'ma lil nigga, but I keep a big ass four-fifth on me," Lil Fif pronounced, lifting his black V-neck T-shirt to show his big pistol.

"Okay…Okay, I'm feeling that. I ain't even gotta ask why they call you shooter."

"You already know, ya heard me," Shooter retorted lifting his shirt to show his pistol. "This our boss man right'cher, and you his sister. So, if you need us for ANYTHING, we on go! Straight demon time ya heard me."

"Already! I see what it is. Just make sho y'all keep my brother well protected and we don't have no mishaps.

"F-sho bosslady." Lil Fif added before him and the shooter returned to their cut in the garage.

"Look, it's five pounds in that trash bag. They for you, you don't owe me nothing."

"That's ..Love..Love you…Sis," Hassan said sincerely.

"Love you too, nigga. Look, I want'chu to meet somebody too."Assata peeked out of the glass sliding doors and waved for G.I. to come in. Moments later, G.I, entered the garage in a matching red Burlington sweatsuit. Even though he was a humble soul, his presence commanded attention.

"Bra, this my friend G.I., G.I, this my brother Hassan," Assata introduced them with an irrepressible smile on her face.

"It's a true pleasure to meet'chu bra. I heard all solid shit about'chu," G.I. stated shaking Hassan's hand firmly. Hassan smiled and returned the firm grip on G.I.'s hand. Nice to…meet'chu..too bra…Shiidd..All this…Time…I thought you..was..damn gay."

Assata laughed.

"Excuse my brother, he a lil sedated," Assata chimed.

"Ain't nothing wrong with it. Just, don't let it control you." G.I, exclaimed. Even though Hassan was under the influence of codeine and high grade weed. He, Lil Fif God, and shooter all could see through G.I''s humility. They knew a killer when they seen one.

"I'm so..glad…you gotta man..Maybe he..Can…Stop you..From being..So damn Violent

"Stop it, Hassan," Assata proclaimed.

"Don't be fooled…by dem big pretty..ass dimples. You…fucking wit.. A cold killa," Hassan stated laughing.

"I know a killa when I see one." G.I. shot back.

Chapter 11
FOUR OF A KIND

Charity was relaxing in the living room on her sectional couch watching Zatima and eating a bowl of butter pecan when there was a knock at the door. She waited a few moments, then got up to see who was disturbing her peace. Charity peeked through the peephole, smiled, and then got up to this open the door in a pair of extra small booty shorts, and a tank top.

"Heeyy, sexy lady. What do I owe the pleasure?" Implored Charity, stepping aside to let Ketta in.

"If you only knew," Ketta replied entering Charity's bachelorette styled home.

"Welcome to my palace," announced Charity closing the door.

"You on ya lil bachelorette type shit, huh?"

"You already know, bitch. I gotta have carte blanche 'round this muthafucker." Charity sat next to Ketta who had already made herself comfortable.

"So, what blew you out this way? You finally decided to switch teams?" Charity teased licking her tongue out. She quickly put her tongue back in her mouth when she noticed the severity of Ketta's expression. "Wassup, wit'chu?" Questioned Charity frowning deeply.

"Pussy ass hoe! Why the fuck you ain't tell me Ken Mascura was gone be at that fucking party?" Charity shrugged her shoulders.

"I'on know, shid...I didn't think it mattered."

"Bitch! That was his house! The fucking sheriff! You got me bringing coke to the fucking sheriff!" Ketta drew her pistol swiftly and placed it against Charity's right eye. "You trying to case me up? You playing with my freedom?" Ketta barked through clenched teeth. Charity raised both of her hands in abdication.

"I'm not tryna bring no harm to you. I swear. I just felt like shit I dig you, why not help put some money in yo' pockets," pleaded Charity.

"Yeah...But all money ain't good money! Na you got me in the bed with this racist ass kracka! I'll be dead ass wrong if I lift yo' scalp in this mothafucka though, huh?" Ketta pushed her pistol deeper into Charity's eye.

"What can I do to make it right?" Inquired Charity.

Ketta removed the pistol from Charity's face.

"Go, get dressed," Ketta demanded.

"What's the occasion?"

"You dun, put me in the bed with this kracka! Hoe, plenty room for you too. We goin' on one. So, dress accordingly."

***

It was a little after eleven p.m. when Ketta reached a dirt road that was two miles away from Ken Mascura's Cocaine Mansion. The street bore no light poles and appeared creepy and desolate. At the end of the dirt roads was a grandiose home with no neighbors. Foreign and old school vehicles were in clusters all over the private property. Ketta parked her rental and readied her weapons.

"Bitch, you ready?" Ketta asked Charity, who appeared a bit nervous.

"Give me a minute," Charity retorted, pulling a gram of coke from her cleavage and taking a bump. Ketta shook her head in disappointment.

"You ready, nah?"

"Yeah, let's roll," Charity retorted, feeling more confident in her ability to perform. Ketta departed from her vehicle with Charity following suit. When they reached the porch, they came to a metal screened door that had burglar bars and a buzzer next to it. Ketta gave Charity an all or nothing gaze, then pushed the buzzer next to it. Moments later, a door opened behind the screened door, and a tall, burly, bald man appeared.

"What can I do for you ladies?" asked the doorman who held a .40 caliber at his side.

"We here to get this, sshmoney daddy," Charity announced seductively.

"It's a $20 dollar admission," the doorman informed.

"That's not a problem," Ketta assured. The doorman popped the door open and let the women in. He gave Ketta a nod, letting her know that he was in on the play. Ketta grinned undaunted, pulled a wet mud brown Glock 31 from her nylon hoodie and wacked the doorman across the chin, surprisingly dropping the six foot three giant. Charity drew her Taurus .380 and aimed it at the doorman.

"Hold me down," Ketta told Charity, tucking her Glock and taking the doorman's belt off to tie him up with it.

"Fuck you doing?" The doorman whispered while Ketta forced him on his stomach, and strapped his arms and legs together. She then drew both of her Glock 31's and proceeded to beat the meat off of the doorman's head until he was unconscious. Charity, not wanting to seem helpless, joined in the onslaught until Ketta stopped her.

She tucked her pistols, and Charity did the same. A commotion could be heard coming from the den that was just around the wall from the living room.

"I got tripps. Nigga you can't fuck with that," Junbug boasted.

"Four of a kind, stupid nigga! Run me my money," Fly countered.

Ketta and Charity made their way into the den. The den was crowded with niggaz at a poker, skin, and dice table. The room grew silent when the two beauties entered the room.

"Damn red! That shit fallen off the bone, ana?" Junbug announced as reference to Ketta's thickness.

"You already know," Ketta retorted then turned around and made her ass clap. Charity slapped Ketta's ass aggressively, and gripped it, drawing all attention to them.

"Damn!" Junbug started grabbing his dick. All in one motion, Ketta spun around with both pistols drew.

BOC! BOC!

Ketta planted two shots in Junbug's chest, dropping him instantly.

"Yall know what the fuck this is! Run that, shit! Everybody against the wall, hands in the fucking air! You buck, you die! Simple!"

Ketta planting three hot ones in Junbug chest got everyone in compliance. Charity pulled a pillowcase from her hoodie and started putting the money from all tables in it. She then made her way around the room, making everybody strip down to their socks, taking cash and jewelry. When Charity made her way to the last victim, he couldn't help himself.

"You bitches know who you fucking with?" asked a dope boy by the name of Fish. After stripping him and taking his belongings, Charity pulled her pistol from her hoodie.

"Do it look like we give a fuck?"

Boc!

Charity drilled a hole in the side of Fish's head, causing blood and brain fragments to scatter about. Her demonstration caused a wave of panic throughout the room. Everyone remained silent, praying not to be the next victim.

"Everybody, on the fuckin ground! Now!" Ketta demanded. Without hesitation, everybody laid on the ground half naked.

"Don't move or say shit in this motherfucka!" Ketta stated then motioned for Charity to fall back and follow her. Both women backed out, guns up. When they reached the front door, Ketta planted one in the doorman's head before their departure. They hopped into the getaway vehicle and vanished into the night under the Florida moon.

Chapter 12
FUCK IT!

When Ketta pulled into Charity driveway, it was a little after one in the morning. Charity took another bump in each nostril, and bobbed her head to Glorilla's Tomorrow 2 Feat. Cardi B.

She the type, tha nigga make her mad, she go and tweet something

Me I'm kinda ratchet still/ so i'm the type to beat something

I can't love you baby like yo' bitch do/So don't leave her

He gone choose her every time/kuz it's cheaper to keep her

Caught up in the moment and euphoric high, Charity doesn't notice Ketta observing her behavior after what she assumed to be Charity's first murder. Ketta turned the music down, grabbing Charity's attention. She now sees the look in Ketta's face.

"Wassup sexy?" Charity asked seductively. Ketta continues to gaze at Charity a few more seconds longer before speaking.

"You, aight?" Ketta implored, killing the engine.

"Yeah I'm good. Why, wassup?" Ketta nodded her head up and down.

"Nothing. Come on, get out. Ketta exited the rental car with the spoliation in her hand with Charity following behind her. Once inside, Ketta sat on the leather sectional, and dumped the proceeds on a coffee table that sat in front of the couch. Charity headed into the kitchen and returned with a bottle of 1800. She got comfortable on a sofa and took shots from the bottle. Ketta scanned over the jewelry counting ten rollies, seven Cuban links all weighing 500 grams busted down, fifteen bracelets, and thirty-seven rings.

After thumbin' through the money, Ketta was looking at two-hundred and forty-eight racks.

"I'on want no jewelry," Charity declared after taking another shot.

"You was hit on that, anyway," Ketta assured, handing Charity twenty-eight racks. Charity chuckled, grabbed the money, then took another shot. Ketta placed everything into a pillow case, then sat back on the sofa staring at Charity.

"Ummmm…Why you keep looking at me like I'm crazy?" Questioned Charity taking another shot and passing the bottle to Ketta. Ketta takes a shot before replying.

"Was that yo' first kill?" Charity nodded with both eyebrows raised.

"I'on believe you. You hit that man with zero hesitation, and you all the way calm as fuck right now." Ketta took another shot. "Ain't no way in hell!"

"Well, first of all, you put a whole gun in my face. That was persuasive in itself. Plus, I felt fucked up for putting you in a situation wit' Mascura. As for me hitting that nigga in his shit, he treated us bad. You ain't hear him?" Charity takes another bump of coke. "Uhmmm!" Charity moans as the coke hits her bloodstream making her pussy wet.

"Yeah, I heard 'em"

"Was that your first kill?" asked Charity, already knowing the answer.

"On or off record?" Ketta retorts egotistically.

'Okay, Shaft," pronounced Charity her voice dripping with sedition while flashing a devilish grin. She slid off of the sofa, stood and removed all articles of clothing.

"Fuck is you doing?" Ketta shouted impulsively while secretly admiring Charity's perfectly sculpted body. Her beautiful black skin was flawless, with a C-cup breast that sat up with no help of a bra. Her stomach was flat, and her pussy was so gorgeous that it looked as if it had never been tampered with in life.

"I'm sorry I put you in a situation. Do you think you could ever forgive me?" Charity asked, falling to her knees in front of Ketta.

"Yeah bitch, we good. Na get up, bitch you trippin!" Charity ignores Ketta's wishes and swiftly snatches Ketta's sweats off. No surprise to Charity, Ketta is not wearing panties. Her mouth waters at the sight of Ketta's fat shaved pussy except for a landing strip.

"I just wanna sho' my appreciation for your friendship" Charity announces placing a tender kiss on Ketta's inner thigh. Her soft succulent lips sends electricity though Ketta's vagina.

"Bitch I told you, I ain't gay."

"I know. You ain't gotta do shit for me, but lay back and enjoy this mouth," stated Charity placing more kisses on Ketta's thighs.

"You know what, fuck it!" Ketta took another shot, then placed the bottle on the table. She raised one of her legs on the couch, grabbed the back of Charity's head and guided her to the place where most men lose their mind.

***

Ketta made it home from Charity around 4:30 a.m. She slept until a little after 8:00 p.m. and was now headed to Ken Mascura's Cocaine Mansion party. Once there, she went through the usual with Bob answering the door, and trying to get fresh with her. After dealing with his antics, she sold him six ounces of coke at three-thousand a piece, and sold another five ounces before she could make it to Mascura.

Thirty-three racks in less than twenty minutes. Not bad at all thought Ketta. When Ketta made it to Mascura favorite spot of relaxation, she wasn't surprised to see another under aged head in his lap.

"Ketta! What's happening, sister gal?" Mascura greets in his heavy redneck drawl.

"Howdy pig" Ketta retorted, having a seat a few feet away from the girl that was pleasing Mascura.

"Come on now. When you talk to me like Kak, you make me feel as if we ain't friends," Mascura countered with his head back.

"This shit bidness, nothing more." Ketta proclaimed with a feeling of disgust.

"Awl now. The way I see it. We are friends. Now, what'chu got for a friend?"

Ketta pulls the money from her Hermes bag and sits it on a table in front of her next to a bowl of coke.

"That's a hunid racks," Ketta assured, standing to leave.

"That's 50 percent?" Question Mascura.

"Yeah."

Mascura chuckled. "I bet. So, where is the dope?" Mascura asked, moaning from the head he was receiving.

"I sold it to your company inside."

Mascura laughs. "I'm not talkin' about that little bullshit you sell my associates. I'm referring to the dope that was in that gambling spot."

"What dope? You didn't mention anything 'bout no dope," Ketta vocalized dubiously.

"I reckon you killed the fella I had planted on the inside before he could tell ya."

"Paper's right here on the table. Have a look." Ketta grabbed the paper, and was sick to her stomach, when she seen the come up she fucked up royally.

"GANG BANGERS GAMBLING SPOT ROBBED AND TERRORIZED! TWO SLAINED WITH FIFTY KILOGRAMS LEFT INSIDE!" Ketta shakes her head in disbelief. Ironically, the only two slayed, were the only one's who knew about the dope.

"Fuck!"

"Yeah, fuck is right." Mascura added. That fifty percent just grew into sixty.

"Fuck you! Aint no extortion playing this way here! You get what the fuck I give you or I'ma blast yo' ass all over social media with these photos of you and these underage girls!" She threatened, showing him the photos on her phone. The underage girl pulls Mascura's little dick from her mouth with worry in her eyes.

"Please don't! MY partners would kill me!" Cried the little girl.

"She's just teasing," Mascura assured, guiding her head back to his lap.

"Now see! You done scared my company. Now you listen and hear me good. You may threaten my associates with that photo crap. But that shit means absolutely didly to me. I'm the king round these here parts. I run this city! You've heard of me, I'm sure of it! I've traded in my sheet for a uniform. But don't ever fucking get it twisted. The clan is still very much alive." Mascura paused and gives his words time to sink in. "You know what your people call, stain? Well, I'm the fucking grand wizard! Head of the Clan!" Ketta's blood is boiling while thoughts of killing him pervade her mine. She turns to leave.

"How's Assata?" Mascura asked. This question caused Ketta to spin around to face him.

"You leave her out of this!" Ketta snaps.

"Sure! All you gotta do is play ball and don't fuck up the capers I send you on. Tell her I said don't spend all that Bahamian money at once."

"Look! I wouldn't give a fuck what rank you hold with that uniform. Or up under that pussy ass sheet you hide under! You fuck wit' my daughter, I'ma sho you what real stain is!" Ketta threatened, then turned to leave.

"Yeah alright! You heard of Rihanna, haven't you? Bitch better have my money!"

Chapter 13
THE JETTY

Ketta sat across from Assata taking shots from a Remy bottle that she snuck into Wing Stop, while Assata devours a twenty-piece chicken, all flats with no sauce. She tried to take Assata somewhere expensive, but she just wanted lemon peppered wings.

"So, how have you been?" Ketta asked feeling good off the Remy.

"I been good," Assata replied before fucking another wing up.

"What about, Hassan?"

"He aight. I know he was still struggling with the loss of Husain, Pops, and being paraplegic. He been using codeine to cope with it, and that shit I don't like," expressed Assata.

"Just see if you can talk to him, you know. When you were in prison, I looked out for him but our relationship ain't like mine and yours. What happened to his girl? She still around?"

"I ain't been seeing her, ma." Lied Asata. A few moments past, giving Ketta enough time to take another shot, and Assata to fuck up a few pieces of chicken.

"I wanted to run something by you," announced Ketta contemplatively.

"Wassup ma?"

"I gotta lot of shit goin' on right na, and I don't want'chu gettin' caught up in my bullshit. So, I wanted to know how

67

you felt about going on a vacation for a while until shit die down." Ketta took another shot while she awaited Assata's reply.

"Look ma. I'on care what'chu got goin on, I ain't leaving you. I'm rockin' out witchu. Come on ma, you know my body."

"Trust me baby, I know, but this ain't no street beef. This shit here on a higher echelon. This some other shit baby," Ketta stated significantly.

"Fedz!"

"That's one of the many entities, but at this moment, no!" Ketta inhaled then exhaled loudly before continuing. "You remember the lick we hit with the Bahamians?"

"Yeah."

"Well, the work we hit for, I been movin' out to this party these white folks are throwing. An associate of mine put me up on it, sellin' ounces three bandz a pop."

"Hell yeah! Shid.. Put me in the mix." Asserted Assta.

"I wouldn't put you in a situation thats gone fuck yo life up forever. Them parties are thrown by Ken Mascura."

"Mascura? The sheriff?" Assata implied, her eyes stretched wide. "You sell coke to the sheriff?"

Ketta shook her head with regret. "Unfortunately. By the time I realized it, I was already knee deep. Na, he semi pressin' me on the extortion tip."

"Man, fuck that Kracka! He can get it!" expressed Assata ready to ride with the mother figure.

"He know too much, Assata. He knew about me, and your father. He even knows 'bout the Bahamians we hit, and threatened to come after you if I don't play ball. Assata, I can't let you get caught up in the twist because of me. Please think about going out of town for a while. Please," Ketta enunciated with pleading eyes. Assata took a moment to process everything before giving Ketta an answer.

"Where exactly is this vacation?" Assata questioned.

"Brooklyn, New York."

"I'on know, nobody in New York," retorted Assata, her face crinkled.

"I have a sister in New York. Arlicia, and she has a daughter your age, her name is Jada."

Assata exhales irritably. "Give me a few weeks to get some shit in order. I'll do it for you, ma."

"Thank you, baby."

"What about Hassan?"

"Mascura didn't mention him, but if he wants to go, that's fine."

"Aight," Assata replied, pushing the rest of her wings to the side. The thought of leaving Hassan and G.I. killed her appetite.

***

Back in Ketta's truck, she continued to take shots from her Remy bottle. Despite her current situation, she was feeling extremely good. A lot of things have been weighing on her consciousness, and she feels that now is the best time to disclose it to Assata in case it goes thick with Mascura.

"Assata," Ketta called out, breaking Assata's trance.

"Wassup, ma?"

"Look under your seat and grab them bags."

Assata reached under and pulled the two bag up. One a brown paper bag, and one velvet. Assata opened the paper bag and seen stacks of blue hundreds.

"That's forty racks," Ketta declared.

"For what??"

"For you, baby girl."

"Thank you ma," said Assata opening the velvet bag."

"Anything for my, baby."

Assata dumped the bag in her lap and found herself gazing at two bust down Cubans, both weighing 500 grams each, two Cuban bracelets, and four Rolex Sky Dwellers.

"What I'ma do with this, ma?" Asked Assata.

"Whatever, sell it, wear it. It's yours," Ketta retorted pulling up to the Jetty.

"Thanks."

Ketta put her truck in park and asked Assata to step out with her. Assata pushed the money and jewelry under the seat and stepped out. Ketta took Assata out by the water, along with her bottle. She took a sip, then passed the bottle to Assata.

"I gotta holla at'chu, 'bout something grave."

"Wassup now, ma?" Assata questioned, thinking shit couldn't get any worse. Tears fell from Ketta's face, causing a palpable sense of fear to fan through Assata's body.

"Ma, wassup?" Ketta exhaled while more tears dropped rapidly from the wells of her eyes.

"It's about your brother, Husain."

"What about'em?"

"I know who killed him." Assata's face instantly expressed malignancy. "I've known this for years, but I kept it in my chest."

"Why did you keep this from me? From my father? Why tell me now? You know what, it don't matter. Tell me who did it, so I can avenge my brother," Assata pronounced seethingly. More tears fell from Ketta's eyes.

"I'm telling you now because I don't know if I'ma make it on the other side of this Mascura shit and I didn't tell you earlier because your father was the one who killed him." Assata dropped the Remy bottle causing it to shatter. She gazed at Ketta in disbelief.

"What type of time you on? Huh?" Assata balled up her fist ready to pounce on the woman she loved. "Why the fuck would you even allow some stupid ass shit like that to roll off yo' tongue."

"Yo' father killed him because he was a rat. Husain had cut a deal with the State for a lighter sentence. He was set to testify against Tasha and your father refused to let it happen.

I pulled some strings to get Husain released but I swear to you, I didn't know yo' father was gone kill 'em."

Assata had a flashback to the day that her father looked her in the eyes and told her that Husain had been killed. Then, flashed off to the slicing of Tasha face for calling her brother a rat played through her mind. She zoned out vaguely, and had no sense of time or space in that moment.

"Assata!" Ketta yelled, bringing Assata back to reality. After analyzing everything, Assata knew Ketta was telling the truth.

"Assata, there's more," Ketta declared sadly. Assata grabbed both of Ketta's arms while tears formed and fell from her eyes.

"When me and your father first started building something, I used to do hits for him. On this particular hit, he sent me to his place of bidness. He never told me why, or who she really was. I read the papers and realized that your father had sent me to kill his significant other. He sent me to kill your mother."

Assata's eyes grew wide as she was filled with heartbreak. Instead of drawing away from Ketta, she buried her face in her chest and wept uncontrollably. She now overstands why Ketta held her down all these years, and regardless of all she'd been told, she still loved Ketta with all her heart. Her anger was directed towards her father.

"I'm so sorry, baby," Ketta expressed, holding Assata tightly.

"I love you so much."

Chapter 14
GOD WHY ME

A week later…

Assata was in her apartment above the Brownstone, laid on her back with her legs spread eagle. G.I. had placed tender kisses on her forehead, down to her patch of happiness and was now headed to an innocent place that no man had ever been.

Assata back arched with her toes cracking simultaneously anticipating G.I's tongue on her love button. She exhaled loudly as her heart rate increased slightly. G.I. placed a kiss on her clit, flicked it three times with his tongue, sucked it a few seconds then blew softly.

"Sss, whoooo…yes!" Assata moaned seductively, turning G.I. on more than he already was. He took his middle and index finger, turned them face up, then slid them inside Assata's goodness.

"Hhhmmm…" Assata groaned, gripping the Versace sheets. G.I. found Assata's G-Spot behind her clit, then proceeded to move his fingers side to side at a rapid pace. Once he seen Assata's reaction, he flicked his tongue across her clit. He continued to hit her G-Spot with his fingers. Assata gripped G.I.'s dreads, threw her pussy upward, and caught a powerful orgasm. The noises that Assata was making could be confused with those of a poltergeist. G.I. removed his fingers and licked them clean, loving the taste.

The site of this caused Assata to come again in extreme bliss. After composing herself, she forced G.I on his back and straddled him. Wasting no time, she lifted herself, grabbed his exceptional nine inches, and guided him to another world. Assata eased down slowly until she had every inch inside of her causing G.I. to moan and curl his toes.

"Sss… fffuck," he cried with clenched teeth. Assata rose slowly, then dropped down rapidly. She continued this routine a few more times, then rose to the top of G.I.'s dick, rode only the head, then eased down on all of him slowly.

"Shit! That's a good girl; ride yo dick!" G.I. coached. Assata leaned forward, licked his nipple, sucked it, and bounced on his dick at the same time. This technique caused a nut to conjure from G.I. 's toes and up his spine. The site of Assata's perfectly peach shaped ass bouncing to a delectable rhythm caused G.I. to lose it. Assata could feel him growing a few inches longer inside her, causing her to climax simultaneously with G.I. Assata continued to ride him slowly clenching her tight pussy walls around him until she was just as empty. She then slipped off of him and laid beside him catching her breath. G.I.'s dick was left limp, wet, and exposed to the cool air. Assata then slipped out of bed to go grab a wet and dry rag to clean her and G.I.'s love organs. After catching the best nut of his life, G.I. was positive that Assata had activated all of his chakras, and opened his kundalini.

"I love you, Assata," G.I. confessed as she laid her head on his chest.

"Oh, yeah?" Assata retorted, rubbing on his six pack." Why you love me, and when did you decide this?" G.I. drew in a lot of air then exhaled.

"I'm most certain, I love you, because I see a lot of me in you. It's like you, my female twin, except no relation. I love you because you are unapologetically you. I love how you make a nigga feel when I'm near you, but its torment when we are apart. When you not around me, I'on even smile the same. It's like, I need you to feel alive. Kuz without you, it's like my existence has no purpose. Assata, you the realest woman I ever encountered and I want this shit forever." G.I. could feel Assata's tears rolling down his stomach. He lifted her chin and kissed her tenderly.

"It's okay to cry, ma." G.I. licked her tears away.

"I love you, too," Assata admitted. "I love you for being patient wit' me and choosing to love me regardless of my perilous, and peculiar ways. It takes a hellava nigga to be able to deal with, and overstand me. I feel like you my male evil twin, except no relation." Assata managed a smile through the pain, then kissed G.I passionately. After breaking away from the kiss, Assata exhaled and laid back on her extra fluffy pillow, and gazed at the ceiling.

"Wassup bae?" asked G.I. sensing something was wrong.

"In a few days, I'm leavin' town, and I don't know when I'll be back."

"Where? And what'chu mean, you don't know when you'll be back?" G.I. imploded confused.

"I'm going to New York for a family reunion." Lied Assata not wanting to put him in her and Ketta's business.

"Oh, okay…kool. So, you'll be gone for a week or two?"

"Hopefully," she countered. "Listen, can you do me a favor, and look out for my brother while I'm away?"

"No question, ma." A few moments passed before Assata spoke again.

"So, you think you ready to tell me about your' mother, father, and sister yet?"

G.I. scratched his scalp, exhaled, then gazed at Assata. "Yeah, we can talk about it."

"You sho'?"

"Yeah, ma, it's whatever for you."

"Okay, but hold on," Assata proclaimed, slipping out of bed and standing. "Sit up, turnaround and close yo' eyes."

"For what?" asked G.I.

"You trust me, right?"

"With my life!"

"Aight then, turn that ass around."

He did what was asked of him. Moments later G.I. felt something heavy being placed around his neck.

"Keep 'em closed, nigga," demanded Assata. She then placed something on both of his wrists. "Okay, open up," Assata commanded excitedly.

When G.I. looked at his neck and wrists, his eyes lit up. He had a massive Cuban on his neck, one on his wrist, and a SkyDweller on the other. "Bae, what the fuck?" G.I. asked excitedly.

"Just a lil' something I wanted to do for you before I leave. Every time you look in the mirror, you gone think of me."

"Thank you, baby," said G.I., grabbing Assata and kissing her deeply.

"Nah, lay down and tell me about yo' family," Assata insisted.

Once they got back comfortable, G.I. spilled out everything. "When I was five years old, my mother got killed coming outta the Elk's lounge. Some niggaz did a drive–by, hitting at some other niggaz, and my mama got caught in the cross fire. After my mother died, my father started treating me different, so we bumped heads a lot. I guess, you know, that pushed me towards the streets. As for my father and lil' sister, they were killed in a robbery a few months ago. My father was a Bahamian drug lord. He supplied the whole tri-county."

Assata's heart rate increased rapidly. She drew in a deep breath and exhaled slowly, trying to calm herself.

"What's wrong, baby?" G.I. asked concerningly.

Assata shook her head. "Nothing. I'm so sorry you had to go through that." Tears fell from her eyes and onto her bare breast.

"Oh, don't trip, ma," G.I. advised, grabbing her and consoling her. "My mother died years ago. I've been made my peace with that. Me and my father were never close, so that's a dubb. The only thing that hurt me was my little sister. I ever find out who did that, may God be wit' 'em."

More tears fell from her eyes. Not because of his general threat, but because of the fact that she was the one behind his pain. "God, why me?" she whispered.

Chapter 15
PUSSY NIGGA!

It was a little after noon when Assata entered Wolly's store. He appeared to be interacting with a customer, until Assata approached and saw that it was a young thief trying to unload some hot jewelry. Wolly looked up and smiled at Assata.

"Assata, how are you, darling?"

"I'm aight. Hey, you. Get the fuck out!" Assata told the youngin' who was dealing with Wolly.

"Who, me?" asked the youngin.

"Yeah, you! Come back later!"

"Assata, what's your problem?" Implored Wolly.

"I ain't gon' ask you again," threatened Assata, pulling a .380 from her Moncler hoodie.

"My friend, come later, please," Wolly pleaded to the youngin' as flashbacks of Assata killing Pooh Daddy in his store replayed in his mind. "I give you a good deal. Come later, please."

The young one grabbed his jewels and made his exit. Assata followed behind him and put the "We're Closed" sign on the door.

Wolly came from behind the counter and locked the door. "Okay, talk to me. What is it?"

Assata placed the pistol back in her hoodie. "Imma ask you something but I want'chu to be careful how you

77

respond. Our friendship depends on it," Assata stated in all seriousness.

"It's that serious?"

"Graveyard!"

"In that case, follow me," exclaimed Wolly, walking behind the counter, and opening his secret room.

"Da fuck?" muttered Assata, gripping her pistol through her hoodie while following Wolly into the room.

"No funny business. Come," said Wolly peeping Assata's movement. Wolly closed the door behind them.

Assata had never seen so many guns and stacks of cash in her life. Even though impressed, she kept her emotions masked.

"If whatever you want to speak about is important, I figured we might as well have a drink," Wolly announced, grabbing a bottle of Casamigos. He poured two shots and handed Assata one. "Salut." Wolly knocked his shot back, and Assata did the same. "You know your father is the only one who has been in this room."

"Lucky me, huh?" Assata uttered sardonically. "Speaking of my father…have you heard from him? Do you know if he's still alive?"

Wolly poured another shot and offered another to Assata who respectfully declined. "Is this the reason you've come?"

Assata remained silent, but her deep-set calculated eyes said it all.

Wolly downed another shot. "Okay. Yes. Your father is very much alive. So is your grandfather. I helped them both escape to Africa."

Assata replayed what her grandmother had told her when she gave her and Hasson the house. Patty, her grandmother, had mentioned going to Africa. "I thought my grandfather died in front of your store," Assata assorted, confused.

"He did flatline, but I was able to haul him in this very room to revive him with the resuscitator, and oxygen tank over there," confessed Wolly.

"Bullshit!"

"No bullshit. Truth only, Assata. The ashes that were spread at the Jetty are only from a barbecue grill. Baby G had created so many enemies, I just took him to a place where he can live in peace, like a king. Khafre, your father, killed two FBI agents. I begged him to leave this country, but he refused. The heat he was bringing was bad for business, so I had my people kidnap him and take him to his father. In Africa. Everything I tell is the truth," Wolly assured with his right hand in the air.

"I appreciate yo' honesty."

"If you ever need *anything*." Wolly empathized waving his hand around the room. "Just say the word."

"You got a number to my father?"

"I do, but you must use a phone that is encrypted. Here." Wolly handed her a phone from the shelf. "Bring back tomorrow.

***

Khafre was a Pharaoh of the 4th dynasty. He had The Great Pyramid at Giza built, leaving one of the most remarkable, indestructible structures in existence. Khafre was overwhelmed with emotion as he stood in front of the pyramids and wept silently with his father beside him. Even though pyramids were built thousands of years ago, the power of his ancestors could be felt through the divine architecture. Wiping the tears from his face, his phone rang. He already knew who it was, being the only one person who had his number. Khafre composed himself and answered the phone.

"Wolly, wassup, Ock?"

It was an awkward silence.

"N'all, nigga, this ain't no fucking Wolly," Assata stated in a dangerously calm voice.

Khafre could tell that the caller was a woman but couldn't determine who. "Ketta?"

"Damn, you don't know yo' own flesh and blood when you hear it?"

"Assata?" Khafre implored excitedly.

"Yeah, nigga, wassup?"

"Baby girl, that's you!"

"First off, pussy nigga, calm all that hype shit down. This ain't that."

"What?" Khafre implored, taken aback by what he was hearing.

"Even though Husain was your son, I can wrap my mind around the reason you put 'em down. A rat is a rat. But, for the life of me, I can't wrap my mind around the reason you had the mother of your daughter killed." Assata barked vehemently.

Khafre exhaled deeply.

"You wacked her out for cheatin'? Aw, man, you's a pussy nigga forreal! I'm ashamed to have yo' blood running through my veins! Ya' father there wit'chu too, huh? Tell 'em I said he pussy wit'chu! Pussy nigga! Stay your pussy ass on that side of the world, 'cause if I catch ya' back this way, I'mma let the song play on yo' bitch ass! Pussy nigga!"

Click! Assata hung up in Khafe's ear, crushing his heart.

Chapter 16
LICK YOU UP, LICK YOU DOWN

Assata hung the phone up feeling somewhat better, having gotten the way she felt about her father off of her chest. She wanted him to know the pain he afflicted had left her with imperishable scars. Assata would much rather kill him, but letting him know that he hurt his baby girl would have to do for now. She kneeled in front of her mother's grave and rubbed her left hand across the expensive tombstone while using her right to pull from the blunt of Zaza.

"Wassup, mama? I miss you; I love you." Assata took another toke from the blunt, then released the smoke from her nose slowly. "So, you cheated on pops, huh?" Assata chuckled lightly. "I guess money really can't buy you love, huh?" She hit the blunt again. "I'on give a fuck what'chu did, mama. That nigga played when he took you from me. A solid nigga don't move like that, ya' hear me? Don't trip doe, I got some shit stewing." Assata took another pull. "Mama, I met somebody. His name is G.I. I love 'em and I know you would, too. I just wish you were here; feel me." She flicked the blunt roach from her fingers and hugged her mother's tombstone.

She placed a kiss on it, stood and turned to leave. Assata walked a few graves over and stepped in front of her brother Husain. "Wassup, nigga? You let pops trick you out'cho life, huh?" Assata shook her head in disbelief. "So, you was a rat?

Tssss… damn, homie. I really ain't got much to say to you, except you played." Assata shook her head, then headed back to her truck. Assata knew that visiting her deceased loved ones on 113 Street put her in death's reach since she'd killed a few of their homies, but she lived for the thrill.

"Psssss….! Psss…! Wassup, baby? Lick you up, lick you down," one of the two youngins called out to Assata as she approached her truck.

She noticed that he couldn't have been no older than fifteen. "Oh, yeah? You gone let me see what that mouth do?" Retorted Assata, prompting the youngins to turn around on their bikes.

Boc! Boc! Boc! Boc!

Assata had drawn her pistol swiftly and let off four shots in their direction, missing intentionally. She knew they had no knowledge of who she was because they didn't come at her guns blazing. For that reason, she decided to spare them, for now. The two youngins swiveled, dropped their bikes, and dug up the concrete trying to get out of death's way.

Boc! Boc! Boc!

Assata let three more shots ring then hopped in her truck and pulled away.

***

"What it's looking like over here?" Assata asked Hassan while he pulled in front of the Brown Store.

"You already know. Traffic look like cattle, nigga," Hassan boasted.

"Shooter and Lil Fif God wit'chu?"

"Every day, all day. Them really my youngins, sis," Hassan stated assuringly.

"So, you trust them young niggaz?"

"Wit' my life, lil sis! I'm all the way up off the demonstration they laid in my lap. Them lil niggaz done put some shit down for me and everything! They solid, lil sis. I stamp that."

"Say no more. I'm handlin' some shit right na, I'ma pull up in a few," Assata exclaimed.

"Fasho."

Click!

Assata jumped out of her truck and headed into the brown store. She caught Wolly pulling up fresh gizzards from the grease.

"Wassup, Wolly?" Greeted Assata.

"Assata, how are you, my friend?" Wolly asked in his deep Arabian accent.

"I'm aight. Here," Assata retorted, handing Wolly back the encrypted phone.

"Your father happy to hear from you?"

"More surprised than anything," retorted Assata. "I needed that, Wolly.

'Thank you."

"No problem, my friend. If you ever want to leave country, I can arrange."

"I'll keep that in mind," assured Assata.

Chapter 17
ITS GETS DEEPER

The traffic was so hectic on Ave S that Assata had to pull into the parking lot across the street from her and Hassan's home. She sat in her truck and watched Shooter and Lil Fif God serve the customers until it died down. Impressed with their movement, Assata hopped out and made her way across the street with a bag in her hand.

"All, hail the Queen," Lil Fif God greeted bowing his head.

"Wassup wit' it," replied Assata.

"Greetings, Queen," Shooter announced.

"Shooter, what dey do?"

"Some shit, different toilet," he countered.

"Y'all fall in here right quick. Let me scream at you," Assata ordered. Shooter and Fif followed behind her into the garage.

"Wassup bra?" Assata asked Hassan, who was smoking a blunt.

"You know the vibe. What's good wit'chu?" Instead of replying, Assata went in her bag and handed Hassan five racks.

"What this for?" Asked Hassan. Assata continued to ignore him, pulled the Cuban from her bag and placed it around his neck.

"Da fuck?" Hassan spat excitedly. She then placed the Cuban and Sky Dweller on his wrist.

Just a lil token of my love," Assata stated finally.

"Damn! This shit heavy! I'm fucking wit' it, sis. Thanks. Who you killed for this shit?" Hassan implored, laughing.

"Don't ask, and I won't tell," Assata retorted reaching in the bag and handing Shooter, and Lil Fif God both Sky Dweller Rolexes.

"My brother vouched for y'all. He speaks highly of you both. This is to welcome you to the family."

"Appreciate chu, Queen," Lil Fif God asserted, snapping the rollie on his wrist.

"Yeah, you are appreciated, Queen," Shooter added, snapping his rollie on. "Hassan is our big bra. We frontline 'bout him. You his sister, the Queen! So, you already know how we comin' 'bout'chu. Say the word and we spinnin' on WHOEVER!" Shooter stated passionately.

"You know the vibe, Queen," Fif added.

"I hear y'all, and I respect that. We'll be rotating together sooner than later. I just wanted to bless y'all, but do me a solid, and let me scream at my brother right quick."

"Say none, Queen," Shooter replied, making his way out of the garage. When Lil Fif God walked past Assata, she stopped him.

"Why they call you, Lil Fif God?" Assata questioned curiously. Lil Fif God laughed before answering.

"Kuz I'ma lil nigga, who keep a big ass four-fifth," Lil Fif explained lifting his shirt showing a big ass .45.

Assata shook her head in approval. "Respect," said Assata cracking a smile. Lil Fif made his way out of the garage to join Shooter.

"Wassup sis?" Hassan asked, confused. "How you gone tell them their family, but you can't speak to me in front of them? How that work?" Hassan questioned feeling more offended than the youngins themselves.

"I'ma pretend that you ain't even say some stupid shit like that. If I told them to excuse themselves, that mean this shit for me and yo' ears only," Assata lectured. Hassan took a pull from his blunt and shook his head in agreement.

"You're right. Wassup though?"

"Hussain, was a rat," Assata mentioned jumping straight into it.

Hassan's face crinkled with confusion. "Wait, wait, wait! Ain't chu the one who put Tasha down. For calling him a rat? Aint 'chu the same muthafucka who killed my bitch, cuz you assumed she knew you killed Tasha? Help me understand this shit, lil sis. That's why you gave me these jewels? What, this supposed to be some kind of guilt gifts?" Hassan ranted.

"Nigga please! I gave you them jewels and money kuz we family, silly nigga! Don't get it twisted, it's still fuck both them hoez! I did what I felt I had to do to protect my freedom."

"Calm down. I'm just stating the obvious," Hassan countered.

"Whatever nigga. Anyway, yo' father was the one who killed him. When he found out, Hussain was testifying against Tasha, he pulled some strings to get 'em out. He picked Hussain up, took him to the "River" and left him in the car." Hassan took in everything he was being presented with and applied it to logic. He knew her father hated rats. To find out he his own son had turned coward had to be devastating to his pride.

"That pussy nigga had my mom killed too. He found out she was fucking another nigga, so he had her put down. Instead of just leaving her, this tender dick ass nigga had her killed," Assata pronounced, her blood boiling at the mention of it.

"Who told you all this shit?" Hassan questioned.

"Don't matter. You know the shit true."

Hassan hit the roach of the blunt then flicked it on the garage floor. He then shook his head in agreement.

"You remember when you were younger. It was like four in the morning, and you walked in pops room and caught me standing over him." Asked Hassan.

"Yeah! I asked you what was you doin' in his room? You said that you was just checking on him. What about it?"

"I was finna kill 'em, but you walked in and saved him."

"Kill 'em for what?"

"When me, and Hussain were babies, pops came to see us at our mother's house. You know me and Hassan were born a day apart from twin mothers. Anyway, I remember them arguing, but I was too young to remember why. I remember pops leaving us in the room with our mothers following behind him. Then moments later, he came back into the room, and grabbed me and Hussain.

Hussain was asleep, but I was awake. When he carried us outta the room, I remember seeing both of our mothers laying on the floor with puddles of what I know now was blood surrounding the bodies. I called out to my mother, but she never answered back," Hassan explained with tears easing down the side of his face.

I been seeing this in my head for years, hoping that it was just a dream. I know better though. That's why he home schooled us. Its kuz he killed our mothers and took us."

Everything made sense to Assata.

"Why you just now telling me this?"

"Kuz, this the perfect time to tell ya," Hassan countered, wiping the tears from his face.

"Our family all fucked up," admitted Assata.

"That's an understatement."

"It gets deeper," Assata added.

"Lay it on me."

"That bitch ass nigga still alive!"

Chapter 18
EXCUSE ME!

G.I. fell in the Brown Store, wearing an all black fitted V-neck, black Maison Margiela track pants, a pair of Adidas 'Pharrell Willimas' Cream Edition sneakers, and all the jewelry that Assata had given him. He headed to the freezer, grabbed a peach tea and headed back to the front of the store to grab a twenty piece of Wolly's infamous chicken.

"Wolly, wassup wit' you?" G.I. greeted.

"How do you do, my friend?"

"Let a nigga get a twenty-piece," G.I. ordered. His phone rang moments later.

"No problem my friend," Wolly assured. "Give me few moments to pull if from the grease."

"Fasho," G.I. pulled his phone from his pockets.

"Yeah, wassup?" answered G.I, turning to walk out of the store for a moment. On his way out of the store, a familiar face stared at him intently.

"Wassup bae? What'chu up to?" Assata asked.

"Hold up for a minute, ma," G.I. said, stopping in his tracks.

"Wassup, homie? You know me or something?" G.I. asked in a calm but threatening manner.

Rudolph raised his hands in surrender. "Aye, my nigga, I ain't on nothing. Just trying to grab some gizzards, my nigga," Rudolph retorted grinning with ill-suppressed satisfaction and snake-like suavity. G.I. kept it moving and stepped outside for a minute.

"Bae! What's going on? You aight? You need me to pull up?" Assata asked concerningly.

"Imagine that," he replied.

"I'm serious, nigga! Where you at?"

"I'm grabbing my chicken out of the Brown store right na! Wea you at? I'm finna pull up."

"I'm at my house on Ave S. If you ain't here in ten minutes, I'm pulling up there. You hear me?" Assata asked in all seriousness.

"You tripping, ma. I'll be there less than ten.

"Aight na. I love you, boy."

"Love you too, Dimples."

Click!

As soon as G.I. hung the phone up, he remembered who Rudolph was. He didn't know him personally, but he'd heard of him, and seen him in traffic. Rudolph was an OG from 13st known for his gun game and getting money. He was a short, cocky light skinned nigga. G.I. headed back in the store, at the same time that Rudolph was coming out.

"Excuse me," Rudolph said in all politeness.

"Nall, excuse me, my nigga," G.I. retorted moving so Rudolph could get by. G.I. moved deeper into this store.

"Your chicken is here, my friend," Wolly confirmed.

"What do I owe you?" G.I. asked, going in his pockets.

"Even ten dollars, friend."

G.I. peeled the money off, grabbed his food and turned to leave. When he made it outside the sun was dying, creating a beautiful architecture across the interminable sky. He admired its beauty before hopping into his BMW. As soon as he put the vehicle into drive, Assata called again.

"Wassup, bae?" asked G.I.

"What did I say?" Assata snapped.

G.I. chuckled, easing his way towards the end of the parking lot. "I'm in the wind my love," G.I. assured Assata when a tinted up Mammoth 1000 Ram Henessey pulled in front of him blocking his path. "Da fuck?" G.I. muttered, reaching in between his seat and console for his pistol.

A Cherokee that had been sitting in the parking lot swiftly pulled up on G.I.'s side with the window dropped. G.I. turned to his left, looking Rudolph dead in his eyes.

Boc! Boc!

The first shot hit G.I. in his nose forcing him to topple backwards. The second shot hit him in the cheek forcing him to lean over. The Ram truck pulled off and disappeared in traffic. Rudolph hopped out, opened G.I.'s door, took the jewelry from his neck and wrist, then got missing. Unbeknownst to G.I. the jewelry that Assata had given him was taken from Rudolph at the gambling spot. Rudolph was the only one in the city with a Cuban that had one side gold and the other side busted down in diamonds. As soon as Rudolph seen G.I.'s neck, he knew the Cuban was his. When G.I. stepped outside to use the phone, Rudolph made a call of his own. Miraculously, G.I. rose holding his nose with blood seeping through his fingers. Wolly came outside of the store to see was G.I. okay, having seen it on camera, but G.I.'s vehicle pulled off abruptly. Vision blurred with his face ringing G.I. drove himself to the hospital but not before stopping by his homie J-Fi to throw his pistol out the window into his yard. When he finally made it to the hospital, he put the whip in park, then passed out on the steering wheel, blowing the horn. A nurse who just so happened to be taking a smoke break peeked inside and seen G.I. covered in a sheer volume of blood.

***

When Assata pulled into the Brownstone, Wolly was posted outside. She hopped out and approached him with worry in her eyes.

"Wolly, I heard shots. You seen my dude? He got thick dreads and is driving a BMW."

"Come inside quickly!" demanded Wolly. Once inside, Wolly showed Assata the footage from inside the store, and the footage of the actual shooting. Assata placed a hand over her mouth as a single tear fell from her eyes. She could see Rudolph's face clear as day. She made him freeze it, then took a picture.

"Bet that up, Wolly. Get rid of that footage," Assata stated.

"Done!" Wolly assured. Assata ran outside, jumped in her truck, and flushed it to the hospital. When she got there, the doctors told her that G.I. condition was serious. An hour later, she was able to see him. Assata's heart ached when she laid eyes upon G.I. condition. He had tubes down his throat, and his nose had swelled to the size of an avocado. The doctor told Assata that the only thing that saved his life was the breaking of his nose as a young teen. He'd gotten in a fight and broken his nose. He never went to a doctor, causing his nose bone to heal into an unusual form. His unusually formed structure kept the bullet from penetrating his brain.

"I'm so sorry, baby," Assata whispered, gripping G.I.'s hand. "I got'chu. I promise."

Chapter 19
THE WRONG NIGGA!

"Damn, cuz. It's been a lil minute since we linked in," Shooter implored.

"Hell yeah. What's been going wit'chu?" Asked the voice on the other side of the phone.

"I just been sack chasing and shit…You know the vibe," retorted Shooter.

"Ain't nothing wrong with it. Shid…What'chu doing right na?"

"Bending corners, looking for that gas."

"Shid, slide through! I got what'chu want, got what'chu need!"

"What's the addy?"

"I'm on 27th. I'm in the same spot."

"Say less!" Shooter proclaimed. Shooter hung the phone up and headed to the trap on 27th Street. It was thirty minutes after midnight when he knocked on the door of the trap house. Moments later, the door opened and Shooter's cousin stood in the doorway.

"Wassup, lil nigga?" Rudolph asked happy to see his little cousin. Shooter dapped his cousin up and hugged his neck.

"You know the vibe, big Kuz. What the fuck is up?" Shooter asked, stepping into the trap with Rudolph closing the door behind him.

"How did you get here?" Rudolph questioned.

"I walked. I'm 'round the corner at his lil bitch house. She is waiting on me and shit, so I can't play. I'm tryna push down in that stuff, ya hear me?" Shooter implored, rubbing his hand together.

"I hear ya. Shid, let me get'chu right then. You can't keep lil mama waiting," Rudolph voiced heading to a table in the kitchen that had a Glad bag full of pounds of loud.

"What'chu got?" Inquired Shooter following behind Rudolph.

"Train wreck. Straight pressure!"

"What the zone going for?" Asked Shooter, pulling out a knot of blue face hunnids.

"I can't charge you, bitch. We family," Rudolph retorted eyeballing the ounce instead of using the scale. "Here."

"Good lookin', kuz. This, more than a zone."

Rudolph waved him off. "Whenever kuz. If I'm here, pull up, bitch. I got'chu," assured Rudolph.

"That's love!"

"Gone na. Go beat lil baby back in," Rudolph encouraged with a smile.

"Aight, I'm outty." Shooter dapped Rudolph up and headed towards the door.

"Hold up, fam." Rudolph stated grabbing his pistol off the table.

"Let me walk you over there. You know niggaz be lurking 'round this time."

"I got it fam, I'm strapped," Shooter replied lifting his shirt. Shooter stepped outside then in the driveway.

"I got it, kuz," said Shooter. Rudolph put one in the head of his 9mm. Clit-clat!

"Fuck that, I'm going."

Lil Fif God appeared from a blind spot on the side of the house and pointed his pistol in Rudolph's face. Out of instinct, Rudolph slapped the pistol downwards.

Boc!

A slug hit Rudolph in the leg. Lil Fif God took off running to the opposite side of which he came. Rudolph took off behind him aiming at Lil Fif's head. Lil Fif bent the corner of the house where it was total darkness.

Boc! Rudolph let off a shot but missed. *Boc!*

Before Rudoph could make his way around the corner of the house, Shooter planted one in the back of his neck, dropping him. Rudolph held his neck and turned over on his back. When he looked up, Assata was standing over him.

"I ain't saying you was wrong for doing what'chu did, but'chu did fuck with the wrong nigga," Assata informed calmly. *Boc! Boc! Boc!* Assata planted 3 hot ones in Rudolph's face then took the Cuban from his neck.

Boc! Lil Fif God planted one in his chest for good measure. The trio then ran to the back of the house and slipped through a hole in the gate that Shooter had used wire cutters to make. They hopped in a vehicle that awaited them and slipped away into the night. Rudolph was Shooter's cousin true enough, but he held no place in Shooter's heart. Rudolph was from the other side and had killed a few of Shooter's homies, so he felt that he owed Rudolph no loyalty. When Assata showed him the picture of Rudolph, he dove at the chance to show her where he stood with her and Hassan.

***

A few days later, the swelling had decreased in G.I.'s nose, and he was now fully conscious. He lay in the hospital bed gazing at the ceiling while the events leading up to his previous state replied in his mind, repeatedly. Caught up in a revenge plot, he didn't notice a card that sat next to his bedside. After staring at it for a few moments, he grabbed it and gave it a read.

G.I.

I was taught to protect what I love, and as we both know,
I love you. Nigga, when I told you that Cuban was a token of
my love ... Thats what the fuck I meant!
Assata

A smile stretched from one ear to another on G.I.'s face. He then saw a velvet bag that was sitting next to the card and grabbed it. Pulling the contents from the bag, he seen that it was the Cuban that Assata had given him. It was saturated in Rudolph's blood. At that moment, he knew Assata had avenged him. "I love you too, ma," G.I. muttered to himself.

Chapter 20
LET IT GO

Ketta and Charity had robbed and killed some Mexicans on Boston Avenue that Mascura had lined up. She changed her clothes and came back on the scene as the lead homicide detective. While examining the carnage that she and Charity had left on the scene, Ken Mascura pulled up and approached the scene.

"Detective, let me have a word with you." Mascura insisted stepping off to the side. Ketta followed up behind him.

"Wassup?" Ketta implied irritably.

"How's everything?" Mascura asked, referring to the bricks of coke that she'd took from the Mexicans.

"Everything is everything."

Mascura spat Copenhagen on the graffitied sidewalk before replying. "Good. Now, get rid of it, and bring me my eighty percent."

"You said sixty!"

Mascura spat again. "Did I? Hmm…well, it's eighty now. You've been relieved for today. Peter's taking over. Gone get outta here, and get my eighty percent," commented Mascura.

Ketta was livid but hid her emotions. "No problem, Boss!" Ketta smirked and made her way to her undercover car. While hopping into the vehicle, she viewed her partner, Peter pulling on the scene. She put the car in drive and drove off. Peter hopped out and greeted Mascura on the sidewalk.

"How are you doing, sheriff?" Peter inquired. Before Mascura could reply, a triple black Trackhawk pulled up with the front and back passenger windows dropped. Shooter and Lil Fif God hung out of both windows, both with two twin Glocks that had monkey nuts and switches on them.

ZZZZZZZZZZZZZZZZZ!

The switches had the Glocks sounding like sewing machines, dropping a hunnid rounds each. Mascura and Peter both were peppered with armor piercing rounds, resembling the scene from the Godfather when Tony got whacked out. After making a movie, Assata got on the gas and disappeared in traffic. Assata had been laying on Ketta to lead her to Mascura. All the love that she harbored in her heart for Ketta, she refused to just sit around and watch Masara extort who she considered her mother. Mascura had to get it, and she was willing to put him down with everything on the line.

***

Ketta, Shooter and Lil Fif God switched whips, then headed to her house on Avenue S. They grabbed their weapons and headed inside.

"Roll something up," Lil Fif mentioned to Shooter. His adrenaline was still on a thousand. Assata closed the drapery in front of the glass windows.

"Yall bring that inside," Assata ordered, leaving the garage and heading inside. Shooter and Lil Fif followed suit.

"Switch y'all clothes. Then, we gone get rid of deez straps. Heading in the living room, Assata spotted Hassan in his wheelchair leaning over.

"You on that shit, nodding out again, huh? Wake yo' ass up nigga!" Assata yelled, putting her hand under Hassan's chin and lifting his head to face her. She noticed the blood that had streamed from his nose painting his shirt red.

"Hassan!" Assata yelled hysterically, now shaking Hassan. Shooter and Lil Fif God made their way over to inspect Hassan's condition.

"Big homie! Big homie, wake up!" Yelled Lil Fif, fearing the worst.

"Bra! Stop fucking playing!" Assata cried with tears already falling from her face. Shooter remained silent though it all. He had been told Hassan to ease up on his dosage of codeine, but he dismissed Shooter's concerns.

"Hassan!" Yelled Assata.

"Let it go, sis. Big bra, gone," Shooter voiced with lamentation. Assata wiped the tears from her face, took a deep breath, then exhaled slowly.

"I know," she admitted.

***

Not feeling up to being around a bunch of hypocrites, Assata thought it best to have Hassan cremated. She spread his ashes at the Jetty with Shooter, Lil Fif, and Ketta accompanying her. Multiple blunts and Remy were in heavy rotation with Hassan's most memorable moments in mind.

"What's next, Queen?" Shooter asked.

Assata hits the blunt before speaking. "Listen I gotta, shoot outta town for a lil minute. I'ma need yall to look out for my people dem, and I assure you, if yall deliver, yall gone be full when I touch back down in the city."

"Yo people, who?" Asked Shooter.

Assata nodded her head towards Ketta who was standing off to the side gazing at the ocean. "Ketta. She is like a mother to me. Protect her like the first lady, ya hear me?"

"Anything, for the Queen. You know that," Shooter said.

"You know we got'cha," Lil Fif God added.

Assata hugged and kissed both youngins on the forehead. "I know. Y'all do me a favor and head to the truck. I'll be there in a few."

Lil Fif God and Shooter obliged at the request. Assata headed over to Ketta and hugged her tightly. Ketta broke away from Assata's grasp and looked deep into her eyes.

"Mascura. That was yo' work?" Ketta questioned. Assata had never lied to Ketta, but felt at this moment, it was necessary. The less she knew, the better.

"I heard what happened to him, and your partner. That wasn't me, but I feel no empathy for him either. Everybody I love seem like they dying off, so fuck that Kraka, ma."

Ketta listened to Assata, but she knew better.

"Well, the city finna be crawling with every agency in existence. Even though Mascura is now a non-factor, I still feel like you should get a way for a while."

"I'm ready," Assata assured.

Chapter 21
GANGSTAZ CRY

When Assata stepped off of the plane at LaGuardia airport in Queens, Ketta's sister, Arlica was there to pick her up. Arlica worked for the NYPD, but doesn't mind getting her hands a little tainted. She also had a daughter the same age as Assata named Jada. After introducing herself, Assata didn't really feel up to conversation. Thoughts of Hassan and G.I. pervaded her mind heavily as she gazed out of the window of Arlica's Audi X6 M series.

'You okay, ma?" Arlica asked Assata.

'I'm good," Assata replied without facing Arlica.

"You hungry?"

"I'm cool."

"You sure, yo? Best hot dogs, and pizza. Word!" Arlicia pitched trying to show civility.

"Maybe later. Don't really got an appetite."

"Okay. Just say when, and I got'chu." Arlicia assured while breezing through Atlantic Avenue. Once they reached Brooklyn, Assata observed how much faster things moved up north. She knew the vibe would be extremely different from down south, so she prepared for the adjustments. Pulling up to 452 on Monroe Avenue, Arlicia parked in front of a brownstone that was connected to more Brown Stones.

"Okay, we're here. You, need help with your things?" Arlicia offered.

"I got it. Thank you, though." proclaimed Assata reaching in the back seat to grab her two duffle bags. When Assata stepped from the vehicle, Arlica's daughter Jada was already approaching.

"You must be, Assata. I'm Jada," she greeted, grabbing one of Assata's bags, displaying a vibrant smile. Assata started to protest, but Jada was swift with her approach, and Assata liked her energy.

"Wassup, with it?" Retorted Assata, following Jada into the apartment.

"Aye yo'! Jada! You seen my Gucci loafers?" Bizzy asked, puffing on a blunt of Gorilla Glue. Bizzy was fucking Jada mom, Arlica. He was a hustler, and held a high rank for the 9 Trey Gangstaz Blood gang.

"Ask my mother," Said Jada.

"Who is that?" Bizzy asked, referring to Assata.

"My cousin, Assata. Assata, this is Bizzy. My mother's thing."

"Aye yo'!, watch your mouth." warned Bizzy, taking a pull from his joint. "Wassup shorty, you smoke?" Bizzy asked, attempting to pass the blunt to Assata.

"I'm cool right na," Assata replied.

"Aight. Anytime shorty, its plenty to go around."

Assata followed Jada to her room.

"I just wanted to show you my room. You can hang out in here as late as you want, but your room is down the hall."

Assata realized that Jada was clearly spoiled rotten. Her room was designer decor from ceiling to floor, and had all sorts of gadgets and appliances. Everywhere. Assata also noticed that Jada loved basketball from the posters.

"Come on," said Jada, taking Assata to where she would be sleeping. When Assata seen when she was to reside, it looked like a carbon copy of Jada's room, just a different design. It was on the second floor of the apartment, and Assata secretly liked it.

"Once you get unpacked, I want to show you around town," Jada said excitedly. Assata gave Jada an evaluative look, and got tomboy vibes from Jada. She had on gym shorts, the latest Jordans and a tank top.

"I just wanna lay down. Maybe tomorrow," Assata suggested, dropping her bag and flopping down on the king's size tempurpedic mattress.

"Okay. I'ma hold you to that. In the morning," Jada sang.

"That's wassup, just wake me up," Assata stated with closed eyes.

"Okay," said Jada leaving out of the room and closing the door behind her. Assata exhaled deeply. She was tired and home sick already. On the verge of dozing off, her phone rang.

"Yeah?" Assata answered dryly.

"Wassup, Dimples? How the Big Apple treating my baby?" G.I. asked concerned. The sound of G.I.'s voice was galvanizing.

"Hey, baby. I miss you already," Assata whined.

"A nigga miss you more. How they treating you though? I need to catch a flight or what?"

Assata managed to laugh a little. "They seem like cool peoples. I ain't been nowhere yet though. It ain't really 'bout me though. How you feeling, you okay?

"Come on nah, Dimples. You know I'm hard to kill." Clowned G.I.

"Okay, Steven Segal. I'm serious though, you aight?"

"Yeah ma! The swelling in my nose went down, and that bullet I caught to the jaw knocked my wisdom tooth out. It's all good though. I spit them bitches out, and kept it moving, ya hear me?"

"I guess. As long as you aight, I'm aight."

G.I. chuckled before replying. "You know you got a nefarious, yet comical sense of humor."

"What'chu referring to?" Assata questioned.

"I got my Cuban on right now and I 'on think I'ma ever take it off. You know, I'm attracted to loyalty and you've proved yours in a succinct amount of time. Assata, you are more solid than any so called homiez I done dealt wit' when it comes down to it. You're bar none. I love you past foreva," G.I. expressed deeply.

A few moments of silence went by until Assata broke it up. She wiped the tears that had streamed down her face. G.I.'s words had touched a place deep in her being. It just felt good to be recognized, appreciated, and loved. She had no brothers, no friends, and now no father. Ketta and G.I. were the closest thing to her heart.

"You my first nigga, my first love. You was patient wit' me, and I respect you for that. You know how I get down, and you choose to love me still. As for that lil demonstration, it's anything for my nigga," Assata expressed.

"Damn, my nigga."

"Wassup?"

"You got tears in my eyes and shit," G.I. admitted.

"Gangstaz cry. Trust me I know 'cause I just got finished wiping my eyes too."

"Me and you foreva! Ya hear me?"

"I'm feelin that," Assata disclosed. The vibe was so genuine and effectual that they talked all night until they both fell asleep while still on the phone.

Chapter 22
FRANK B

It was well afternoon when Assata awoke from her beauty sleep. Looking over at her phone, she seen that it was still someone on there.

"Hello," Assata spoke into the phone groggily.

"Top of the morning, Queen," G.I. muttered.

"Nigga!" You still on the phone?" Assata smiled impressed.

"Yeah! You were snoring and shit." G.I. chuckled.

"Whateva nigga, I don't snore.

"It was a lil cute snore through, bae. I took a shower and everything. You snored the whole time too."

"You took the phone in the shower wit'chu?"

"Yeah, I wanted to be the first one you hear when you wake up."

"That's deep. You think you know what'chu be doing to me?" Assata asked seductively.

"I gotta pretty good idea." G.I. chuckled. But listen though, gone head on and hitcha mouthpiece, then jump in the shower. Get all the goodness together, and I'ma call you later."

"Okay baby, I love you."

"Love you more."

Click!

The moment Assata placed her phone down, Jada entered the room full of energy and flopped down in the bed next to Assata.

'Girl, I been in here three times trying to wake you up for breakfast."

"I was on the phone wit' my nigga all night. I'm tired," Assata stated wiping boogers from the corner of her eyes.

"It's okay. I put you a plate in the oven," Jada announced, rubbing her hand through Assata's dreadz.

Assata removed Jada's hand from her hair.

"Thank you."

"You welcome."

Jada laughed at Assata's bluntness.

"Yeah, I'm into women," Jada admitted smiling, showing her pearly whites that bore gold braces. Jada was 5'9, light skinned, and had three long braids in her head. Two on the side and one in the back. Assata had to admit that even though Jada was a tomboy, she was still attractive.

"I ain't judging you, but I ain't that," Assata exclaimed.

"I'm not trying to turn you out. I think you're pretty and all, but I'm just being friendly. Nothing more yo. My moms and Ketta are sisters, so I want to make sure you good yo'. That's it." Jada assured.

"Respect," Assata retorted.

"Bathroom is down the hall. After you get situated, come downstairs so we can get shit popping for today."

"I'll be down in a few," exclaimed Assata.

"Kool," Jada replied heading downstairs.

Thirty minutes later, Assata descended the steps wearing a tight-fitting Nike sweatsuit and a pair of beef and broc Timbs that Ketta had bought her. She noted Jada playing a PS5 and was about to approach her when Bizzy waved her over. Caught up in the video game, Jada never noticed Assata come down. Assata followed Bizzy outside and stood on the step.

"Yo, here." Bizzy held a blunt out for Assata to grab. She grabbed the blunt and took a pull from it.

"What part of Florida are you from?" Bizzy asked Assata.

"Fort Pierce," retorted Assata, noting multiple teardrops under both of Bizzy's eyes. Bizzy stood 5'6, light skinned, shoulder length dreads, and had Blood Gang tattoos everywhere. Assata passed the blunt back to Bizzy.

"Y'all got Bloods out there?"

"Yeah we got 'em."

"Any Billys out there?"

"What'chu mean?" Assata implored not understanding.

"Nine Trey Gangstaz," Bizzy informed blowing smoke from his nose and passing blunt back to Assata.

"I'on know about all that. We got bloods though. We mainly bang blocks down my way."

"So, what made you come to the town?" Bizzy asked curiously.

Assata exhaled deeply before responding. "I was making too much noise in the city, so my people thought it best to come this way till shit blow over," Assata explained.

Bizzy laughed. "Damn shorty! You putting down demonstrations like that?"

"So they say."

"So they say, my ass! Aye yo' ma! You too cute to be putting in work and all of that. While you down here, just relax and enjoy the town. Welcome to Brooklyn." Bizzy handed Assata the blunt then stepped off the stoop and headed to the trunk of his Rover. Assata stepped down behind him, but didn't approach his truck. She walked up the street a little bit and just took in the ambience. Assata noted how close the brownstone apartments were and how stale the air was. She hit the blunt, then turned around and viewed Bizzy grabbing what appeared to be designer bags from the trunk. Reaching in the truck, Bizzy seen a hooded figure out of his peripheral approaching quickly.

Having left his gun inside, the only reaction he was able to demonstrate was to duck slightly, and raise his right arm using the bag to cover the right side of his face. *BOC!* The first shot went through the Prada bag missing the back of Bizzy's head by inches. The shooter already knew how Bizzy got down, so he was shooting scared. He ran past Bizzy with his gun pointed behind him firing off wild shots. *BOC! BOC! BOC!* One of the shots managed to hit Bizzy in his right ass cheek. Scared to death and not paying attention to what's in front of him, Assata tripped the assailant. He crashed face first into the pavement, dropping his gun. Without hesitation, Assata mashed her beef and broc Timbs in the back of his head, knocking him unconscious.

"Bitch ass nigga!" Assata yelled as she proceeded to crush his head. Bizzy had limped over and picked the pistol up.

"Fall back ma, I got 'em yo," pronounced Bizzy, rolling him over.

"Frank B?" Bizzy recognized with a screw face. *BOC! BOC! BOC! BOC!*

"Punk mothafucka!" Yelled Bizzy planting four hot ones in Frank B's face. Jada came rushing out of the apartment.

"Bizzy! You good yo?"

"Yeah, get Assata outta here!" Bizzy ordered then jumped in his Rover and left the scene. Jada quickly locked the apartment up and ran to her Jeep Cherokee.

"Come on, yo!" Jada called out to Assata who was still standing over Frank B. Assata snapped out of her moment and hopped in the Jeep with Jada. They pulled off and got missing in the Rotten Apple.

Chapter 23
EXACTLY THAT

Three Days Later...

Jada and Assata pulled up to Marcy Projects to visit her sister, Dominique. When they stepped out of the whip, Assata was in awe to see that the project building was seven stories high. Back home, she was used to seeing two stories at the most. It was hustlers, thots, and kids playing on the monkey bars out front.

"What's popping, Jada?" Asked a young rapper by the name of World.

"Us never them," Jada retorted, throwing the Bs up. Jada wasn't affiliated, but being around Bizzy had rubbed off on her.

"All the time!" World replied, eyeing Assata the whole time.

"Peep though, who shorty wit'chu?"

"Fuck you asking her for, nigga? I'm right here." Assata snapped.

"Damn shorty! Little spicy thing, huh? Where you from?" World inquired.

"Killa Kounty."

"Killa Kounty. Where?"

"Fort Pierce, Florida."

"Floridian, huh? Well, welcome to the town. You need anything at all, say word," World announced moving all animated like.

"I'm straight." Assata assured, pushing past World to follow Jada into the project building. Assata noted niggaz by the staircase shooting dice and talking shit. They pushed past the riff raff and headed to the elevator.

"Aye yo! Shorty, with the round bubble!" Called out a stick-up kid by the name of Finesse.

"She good, yo!" Jada yelled over her shoulder. Stepping into the elevator, Assata saw that a light was out, and it smelled of piss from multiple bodies.

"Damn, this shit foul as fuck!" Assata complained.

"This the projects yo. You'll get used to it," said Jada stepping off the elevator onto the third floor.

"I doubt it."

Jada laughed at Assata. "Your projects must be like, mad clean yo," Jada stated stepping in front of an apartment and knocking five times.

"Shid…My shit fucked up, but we don't have hallways and elevators full piss and shit. Our projects don't have elevators period."

The door opened, and Jada's sister, Dominique stood parrot toed with her hands on her curvy hips. Her hair was in butterfly locks, her nails matched her toes, painted to perfection, and her sexy chocolate skin was dipped in a Burberry catsuit.

"This must be Assata." Dominique assumed.

"What makes you say that?" Jada inquired, stepping inside the apartment with Assata behind her.

"Because Bizzy been talking about her all morning," Dominique pronounced.

"Assata, this is my sister, Dominique. Dominique, Assata," Jada introduced.

"I heard good things about'chu. Nice to meet chu yo." Dominique reached out to shake Assata's hand. Assata shook her hand with a half-smile.

"Wassup wit' it?" Retorted Assata.

Dominique chuckled, putting her hand over her mouth. "Yo, your Florida talk is the bomb. Word," Dominique admitted.

"Whatcha mean?" Assata asked confused.

"I like you. That's all I'm referring to."

"That's wassup," Assata said nonchalantly.

"Aye yo! Leave her alone, man. Go ahead! Assata come here, ma." Bizzy exclaimed.

"Fuck you, Bizzy! This my fucking house!" Dominique argued.

"Who pay the bills around this mothafucka!" Bizzy countered.

"Whatever, nigga!" replied Dominique storming off to her room. Jada followed Assata over to the kitchen table where Bizzy sat, smoking a blunt of exotic.

"Wassup, ma? You made it inside the building okay?" questioned Bizzy, passing the blunt to Assata.

"Yeah, I'm Gucci," Assata assured.

"World and Finesse was hounding her yo', but she handled them niggaz." added Jada.

"Oh word?" Bizzy implored.

"You know how them niggaz move," Jada exclaimed.

"Yo, you wanna drink or something?" Bizzy offered.

"What'chu got?" Assata questioned.

"Henny."

"Yeah, let me get a shot."

"Aye yo' get her right," Bizzy told Jada. "Excuse me for a minute," Bizzy stated then slid in the back room.

Jada poured Assata a shot.

"What'chu think of Bizzy?" Jada asked.

Assata shrugged. "He seem like a good nigga," Assata replied.

"Bizzy is big on loyalty. He will go all out for you, if he fuck wit'chu. If you on the other side of his wrath, it gets really dark for you. Word!"

Bizzy appeared from the back room in a red and black Gucci flannel shirt, some black Gucci jeans and a pair of red Prada sneakers. His shoulder length dreads swayed as he walked with a slight limp, due to being shot.

"Aye yo, Jada, hold it down until we get back, ya heard. Assata come with me for a minute."

Assata downed her shot, placed her cup on the table and followed behind Bizzy. He exited the apartment and walked directly across the hall to another apartment, placed a key in the door and entered with Assata behind him.

"I'm just checking something right quick," Bizzy informed.

"I ain't tripping," Assata assured.

When Bizzy made it in the kitchen, he spotted his uncle named Born and his uncle's bitch, Feleica slumped over in a brick of Fetty Wap that they were supposed to be bagging up. Bizzy slapped Born in the back of the head.

"Aye yo! What the fuck!" Bizzy snapped grabbing a newspaper that was folded on the table. He brushed the fent from off the side of Born's face and neck.

"Gimme my shit! Wake the fuck up, yo!" Yelled Bizzy who did the same to Felecia. Assata couldn't hold her laughter. She was astounded to see Bizzy more concerned with the Fent than the wellbeing of whoever the people were. After a bunch of yelling and shaking of the bodies, Born and Felicia became somewhat conscious.

"Get the fuck out, yo! The both of you, get the fuck out, now!" Yelled Bizzy, yanking Born and Felicia up by their clothing.

"This is my motherfucking house, Bizzy. Fuck you!" Felecia stated heavily sedated.

Smack!

Bizzy slapped her upside her head, and threw both of them out of the front door.

"Aaye yo! Next time you motherfuckas dibble in my shit, I'm a kill the both of you! Word to my mother!" Bizzy slammed the door in their faces. "These mothafuckas crazy!" Bizzy snapped, pulling his phone out.

"What was that?" Assata implied.

"My fucking crack head uncle, and his bitch. They gone make me fuck around and let the song play around this motherfucka! Pardon me for a minute," said Bizzy who then spoke into his phone.

"Aye, yo! Come to the spot and get this right for me."

"Say less," replied Lil Blood who was one of Bizzy's scraps.

"Yo, hurry up!"

Click?

Bizzy pulled out a pack of Newports and offered Assata one.

"I'm good."

Bizzy fired one up, inhaled then exhaled.

"You aight?" asked Assata.

"Yeah man, these mothafuckaz yo. It's always something," Bizzy spat seethingly.

"I hear you but'chu already know who you dealing with." Don't let that shit rent space in your head, Big Homie. Relax and keep that shit pushing," voiced Assata. Bizzy gazed at Assata letting her words simmer around his mental.

"You right, yo," Bizzy admitted. "That shit you did the other day was some thorough shit. Word! You ever need anything you say the word and it's handled. Word to my mother," Bizzy exclaimed putting the cigarette out in an ashtray on the table.

"I did what I was supposed to do. Don't let my appearance fool you. I'm with all the bullshit," Assata conveyed.

Bizzy smiled impressed. "Talk yo shit, ma."

There was a knock at the door. Bizzy excused himself and left to open the door.

"What's popping?" Bizzy implored.

"Us never them," Lil Blood replied, peacing Bizzy up the way Bloods do when greeting a homie.

"All the time."

"Woop," Lil Blood counted walking into the apartment. Bizzy closed the door and followed behind Lil Blood.

"Damn! Yo', who shorty is? What's popping, ma?" Lil Blood uttered, eager to find out who the beautiful woman was standing in the spot.

"Aye yo! Fall back, this ain't that! Get'cho ass to that fuckin table and bag that Fetty up! Yo' Assata, let's roll. We out."

Assata made her way over to Bizzy, with Lil Blood gawking her the whole time. Assata went ahead of Bizzy and stood in the hallway.

"She too gangsta for you anyway, lil nigga." Bizzy clowned.

"It's like that?" Lil Blood inquired, eyebrows raised.

"Exactly that!" Bizzy retorted, walking out of the apartment.

Chapter 24
WELCOME TO FORT GREEN

When Bizzy and Assata left the apartment, he took her out to the roof of his project building.

"What's poppin'?" Greeted Wild Blood, who was one of Bizzy's scraps.

"Woop!" Spud greeted, who was also Bizzy's Blood Drop. Bizzy peaced both gangstas up.

"What's poppin'? This the homie, Assata, Assata these some of my drops, Wild Blood and Spud." Both gangstas spoke to Assata and she reciprocated. Assata also noticed the two gentlemen who were trying to shoot their shot at her earlier.

"World! Finesse! What, the fuck is up with'chu niggaz?" Asked Bizzy, dapping them both up.

"What's good, homie?" Retorted World.

"Wassup, man?" Finesse added.

"Yo, let me hit that weed, son." Bizzy implored, reaching for the blunt. World passed Bizzy the blunt, stealing a look at Assata. "Fuck is the vibe? Y'all out here just chilling?" Bizzy asked, walking to the edge of the roof to see what was down below.

"Aye yo'! World! Ain't that ya man?" Bizzy asked, waving World over.

"Son bugging the fuck out, yo!" World goes to the edge to view who Bizzy was referring to.

"Who you talking about, son?" World inquired.

114

"Right there!" Bizzy pointed then quickly pushed World off of the roof.

"Yoooooooooooo!" World yelled all the way down before his body illustrated a bloody decor on the pavement. Out of instinct, Finesse tried to turn and run, but Wild Blood put him in the yoke.

"Where are you off to?" Bizzy asked Finesse while Assata watched in amazement. She'd seen a lot of death, but never seen a man thrown off of a roof seven stories up.

"Let'em go, Wild Blood," Bizzy ordered, pulling a 9mm from his waist.

"What the fuck you runnin' for? Huh? You did something wrong?"

"Bizzy, what the fuck man? All I did was speak to her man. That's it," cried Finesse.

"I heard something different, mothafucka! You fuckin' fifth grade punk!" Bizzy spat shoving a gun in Finesse's mouth. "Yo' it's your call ma. Wha'chu want to happen to his nigga?"

Assata grinned. "I'on see no reason to keep 'em around," she exclaimed.

Bizzy snatched the gun from Finesse's mouth.

"Jump mothafucka!" Demanded Bizzy.

"Come on, man!" Finesse begged.

Boc!

Bizzy shot Finesse in the shoulder. "Jump or the next one's to the fuckin face!"

Finesse made his way over to the edge and jumped.

BOC! BOC! BOC! BOC! Bizzy sent a few shots down with him for the hell of it.

"Punk Mothafucka!" Bizzy yelled then motioned for everybody to follow him to the next building. The trio jumped to the next building over. They departed separately. Wild Blood, and Spud hopped in an AMG, while Bizzy and Assata jumped in a Porsche truck.

That was some wild shit, my nigga. Like, for real though," Assata stated laughing.

"Yo' that's what's gone happen to any mothafucka that disrespect you! Word! I respect that shit you did for me the other day."

"It's all love, my nigga," Assata retorted then her phone rang.

"Pardon me," said Assata answering the phone. "Wassup?"

"Hey, baby girl. How you like it up top?" Ketta asked Assata.

"It's interesting. Different, but interesting."

"I know. It takes some getting used to but just stick it out for a while until shit dies down. And, don't be up there gettin' yo' body count up. Relax, and get'cha mind right," advised Ketta.

"I hear you, but I'ma play it however it come, ma."

"I understand," Ketta assured.

"Oh yeah! I'm fucked up 'bout them lil niggaz. They wit' all the bulshit! You already know I got 'em in motion," Ketta stated excitedly.

Assata laughed impressed with how her proteges was moving.

"Hell yeah, dem my fucking lil niggaz. Send my love."

"They gave me some money to send you. I told 'em you were straight, but they insist. Check ya Cash App."

"Will do, ma. Listen, I'm on something right na. I'ma hit'chu later, ma."

"Okay baby, love you," exclaimed Ketta.

"Love you, more ma."

Click!

"Who was that, moma love?" Questioned Bizzy

"Yeah, yeah, you can say that."

"How you mean?" Bizzy implored curiously.

"My biological mother was killed. Arlica's sister, Ketta took me in as her own. So, yeah that's mama love," explained Assata.

"No doubt. Wassup wit'cha pops? He's around?"

"I' on wanna talk about, fool," Assata retorted, gazing out of the passenger window.

"Say no more," Bizzy pronounced, giving Assata a once over before laying his eyes back on the road ahead of him.

"Where we going?"

"Relax. You wit' me today. Jada will be aight until you get back."

Assata didn't reply. She just laid back into the butter soft, red leather seat, and took in the ambience of New York.

***

When Bizzy pulled into the Fort Greene Projects, three of his female drops were already posted awaiting his arrival.

By their attire alone, one could tell that the trio was affiliated.

"Yo' step out wit' me. I wanna introduce you to my peoples," pronounced Bizzy, stepping out of his Porsche truck. Assata stepped out, and stood by the truck, observing her surroundings. The three women approached Bizzy and formed a shield of protection around him as if he were the president.

"What's popping?" Bizzy greeted, peacing all the women up in tandem.

"Us, neva them!" Retorted Lady, who was a light skinned beauty with long natural wavy black hair. She was dipped in a red Givenchy hoodie, some long black tights that had slits in them exposing her thick blemish free thighs and a pair of red Balenciaga sneakers.

"All, the time," B-Baby added, who was a brown skinned beauty with tattoos all over her curvaceous body and face. The braces in her mouth were red, a beauty mark sat at the right side of her lip, and across her right temple bore the words Blood Love. B-Baby was 5'7 dipped in a red Saint Laurent hoodie, a black pair of tight fitted jeans with slits in them and a pair of red Chanel Sneakers.

"Tamu, Damu!" Mama Blood greeted who was a dark jet-black beauty with pretty white teeth. Mama Blood was a thick amazon dipped in a tight red Versace sweatsuit, and a pair of red Dior sneakers. She held the most stain out of the three.

'Yo, peep this," Bizzy said to Mama Blood as they stepped off to the side. B-Baby and Lady maintained security while Bizzy walked and barked with Mama Blood. Bizzy motioned for Assata to walk with him.

"Aye yo, I just put the nigga Frank B down, so stay 050. Anything close to him, is a plate," Bizzy explained.

"Say less," Mama Blood retorted, eyeing Assata.

"Yo' this is Assata. The nigga Frank B almost got away, but she did her thing, enabling me to do my thing. Word!" Bizzy explained with admiration. "She most definitely, thorough."

"Wass poppin', shorty?' Mama blood implored.

"Wassup wit' it?"

"If the big homie vouched for you, then you gotta be that, yo. Word! You family now."

"That's all, love," Assata replied nonchalantly.

"Wass ya blood type, yo?" Mama Blood questioned referring to what bloodline Assata was bred from.

"Yo, she ain't come home yet, but we'd definitely changing that real soon," Bizzy interjected smoothly.

"Come home?" Assata implied with her eyebrows raised.

"Yo, don't worry about that. We'll bark about that later. In the meantime, welcome to Fort Green. These are my projects," Bizzy boasted using his hands for emphasis.

Chapter 25
DOIN TOO MUCH

It was a beautiful night back in Fort Pierce. The light breeze was soothing, the moon was full, and the traffic was mild. Tod and his sister, Yazmin were parked on the curb on 14th and Ave D in front of the Chinese Rice Hut debating on what to order.

"Yaz, stop playing and tell me what'chu want! I got this lil eater I'm tryna get to. You holding me up," Tod complained.

"Nigga, who come first? Yo' sister, or them lil eaters?" Yazmine questioned with sass.

"Don't make me choose."

"Stop playing wit' me!"

Tod laughed. "You can't make my toes curl! I'm tryna hang out, and you cock blocking!"

"You know what…Nigga just get me a 20 piece of flats, no sauce, with combination rice. Oh, and a peach apple Snapple! Don't forget my Snapple, nigga!"

"Yeah, yeah man! Damn!" Tod barked exiting the vehicle agitated with his sister.

"He gets on my damn nerves!" Yazmin yelled watching her brother enter the rice hut. She grabbed her phone and browsed through Facebook. He just be doing too much, with his sexy ass," Yazmin pronounced, licking her tongue out. She liked Khufu's post, then caught a shadowy figure out of her peripheral. Taking a glance at the rearview mirror, she noticed a hooded individual standing behind her vehicle.

BOC! BOC! BOC!

The first shot shattered the rear-view mirror, causing glass to scatter about, some finding its way to Yazmin's eyes. The other two shots penetrated her back.

BOC! BOC! BOC! BOC! BOC! BOC!

Yazmin screamed in horror while multiple shots found their mark in the shoulder, lung, and spine. Tod finally made his way outside the rice hut and rushed to the vehicle, only to find his sister slumped over; she was still very much alive, but slumped over and paralyzed. The hooded assailant had disappeared into the night unseen.

***

After hitting a few fences, G.I., hopped in a whip that they had a couple streets over, and pulled off. He fired up a blunt of Banana Haze that was in the ashtray, and replayed the movie he had just made. G.I.'s intention was to catch Rudolph's cousin coming out of a trap house that was behind the Rice Hut, but once he spotted Rudolph's sister Yazmin sitting in her vehicle alone, he had to eat. He could have hit Tod before he went into the Rice Hut, but he wanted to drop that pain on him before he decided to kill him too.

***

Niggaz dropped that change on me? I really ain't give a fuck forreal
Y'all niggaz not tough forreal/thuggin its a must I kill
I can quit today, but I'on think the game will love me still/
I tried everything to ease my pain/I'on think nothin' will
Ridin wit' something that spit 7.62's? Like i'm from Summer Hill

I won't leave no trace/put on my mask and gloves before I kill

The sounds of EST Gee's *Forreal* serenaded the inside of a 2019 Chrysler Van that Ketta, Shooter, and Lil Fif God were traveling in. Shooter and Lil Fif God were already killers. EST GEE's murder music was just an extra facilitator for what needed to be done. It was a little after two a.m. and I-95 seemed desolate, all except the trio, and another van.

"Y'all lil niggaz on point?" Ketta asked.

"Come on, ma," Shooter retorted, grabbing a M10 that held a box clip of 250 rounds.

"Pull up," Lil Fif God added, grabbing a weapon identical to Shooter's. Ketta pulled along the side of the van that held a family. She pressed a button that opened the right side of the van. Shooter and Lil Fif pointed their weapons at the other van, barking orders for them to pull over. The driver tried flooring it, but Ketta stayed right along the side of him. Shooter let off a few warning shots prompting the terrified man to slow down and pull over on I-95. Shooter and Lil Fif jumped out maneuvering tactical around the vehicle.

"Get the fuck out!" Yelled Shooter. The driver exited the vehicle with his hands up.

"Please, don't hurt my kids," begged the driver. Shooter forced him to lay on his face. First, alongside his wife and two daughters who Lil Fif had already laid down.

"Mommy, I'm scared," cried one of the little girls.

"It's okay, baby. Hold mommy's hand. The mom grabbed both of her daughters' hands, one on each side of her. Ketta went straight to the trunk of the van and grabbed the shopping bags that appeared to contain canned goods, then put them in the van. She then made her way over to the driver and stood before him.

"Bob! How they been treating you over at the Cocaine Mansion?" Ketta implied with a devilish smirk.

"You don't have to do this. Please, just take the drugs and leave me and my family alone," Bob pleaded. Ketta chuckled.

"I asked your brother, Mascura the same shit. He threaten my people, so it's only right that I match his energy. I refused to be oppressed," Ketta exclaimed. A vehicle slowed down to be nosy.

"What's going on?" Shooter rushed the vehicle and dumped multiple rounds in it, killing its occupants.

"Eat!" Ketta ordered. Lil Fif God went down the line and executed the whole family. The daughters died holding their mothers' hand. Charity was fucking Bob at the Cocaine Mansion. He would get high and tell her everything. Bob told Charity about the cocaine runs he had been going on since Mascura's death. Charity relayed this information to Ketta, and Ketta formulated a plan to execute.

Chapter 26
THAT WAS CUTE

"Woooop!" Mama Blood greeted loudly. All her blood drops responded in kind, throwing up Big B's. Bizzy and Assata stood off to the side smoking a blunt, taking everything in.

"Listen up!" Mama Blood yelled, grabbing everybody's attention. "I'm disappointed in alot of you niggaz, Blood!" She exclaimed pacing back and forth. Most of her drops tried hard to pay attention to what she was saying, but the sweatsuit she was wearing hugged her wide hips and fat ass remarkably.

"That kitty came up short this month, yo!" Mama Blood informed stopping in front of one of her drops.

"Spud! Wass poppin'yo!"

"Was popping, Mama Blood?" Spud retorted nervously.

"You feeling like you're bigger than the nation?"

"Never, Mama Blood! 300, always forever!"

"Then, why the fuck you felt the need not to contribute that baby love to the Kitty this month?" She spat gazing Spud deep in his eyes.

"Mama Love was short on rent, so I used that baby love to make sure she good," Spud explained. Mama Blood shook her head up and down in understanding.

"That's understandable! You not informing me, ahead of time is not! Next month, you double that baby love!"

"050!" Spud replied, letting her know that he's on point.

"Junebug!"

"Wass popping?"

"Nigga, you know wass poppin yo! Everybody was given a hundred bundles with sixty-forty split! Six thousand for the Kitty, four thousand you keep! You put three in the Kitty nigga! Where the fuck that baby love at yo?"

Junebug stuttered trying to formulate a lie, but Mama Blood cut him off.

"You in violation homie! D.P. this nigga and give 'em a lil boy pack until he learn to stand on business!" Mama Blood ordered. Three Blood drops by the name of Despo, Mocho, and Rum latched onto Junebug for 31 seconds, blacking his right eye and busting his lip. They all peaced him up afterwards. Bizzy observed Assata taking their way of life into perspective.

"Kells!" Yelled Mama Blood, .

"What's poppin?" Kells responded comfortably.

"Black Wall Street!"

"Revolutionary reflection !"

"Wooooop!" Mama Blood chanted. "How you feeling yo'?"

"You already know, Godfather flow," Kell stated, conversing that real G's don't die.

"Godfather flow, huh? I hear that but you mind telling me why the fuck you telling Billy business to them Brim niggaz?"

"What?" Kells implored, his heart rate accelerated.

"Oh, you can't hear? Buck fifty this nigga yo!" Mama Blood demanded. A drop named Wild Blood hit Kells across the ear with a scalpel detaching it completely from his head. He grabbed the side of his head and lamented. A drop by the name of Drama drew a P-89 9mm Ruger from his Amir jeans swiftly and planted two holes in the side of Kells head dropping him roguishly.

"Treason will not be accepted! It is and always will be punishable by death!"

"Wooooppp!" Everybody yelled in unison.

"Take this bitch ass nigga to the chop shop yo!" Mama Blood ordered.

Bizzy looked at Assata to view how she was taking the situation. Assata was impressed but repressed it. A few of the members drug the body of Kells to a room to be dismembered and placed in acid.

"Yo, how you feelin'?" Bizzy asked Assata, passing her another blunt.

"I ain't gone Kapp, I'm fuckign wit' it,"Assta admitted

"Listen ma, I admire how you move. I wanna extend my hand and love and offer you a spot in the nation. What'chu think?"

"I accept. What's next?" Assata inquired.

Bizzy smiled reputedly.

"Swooop!" Bizzy yelled.

"Wooooop!!" Everybody retorted.

"To the roof!" Bizzy demanded. Everyone except Drama and Wild blood headed to the roof. Bizzy and Assata were last to join the others on the roof. A circle had already been formed and Bizzy led her to it.

"Do you, ma!" Bizzy encouraged her.

"Assata!" Mama Blood called to the middle of the circle. When Assata entered the circle, the Bloodettes were waiting to blood her in the name of Red Bone, Lady Red and Black.

"Wasssup?"

"Listen, the three of them about to Blood you in for thirty-one seconds," Mama Blood informed.

"What's so significant about thirty-one?" Assata questioned curiously.

"O-Trey-one?" The O is for the U.B.N., United Blood Nation, the thirty is for the laws that we live by, and one is for one Blood Love. That also explains it being three of them, and one of you. Don't sweat it though. I'll pour you a drink on our way of life, gradually. For now, I'ma need you to recite this oath before we get it poppin!" Mama Blood handed Assata a piece of paper to recite the Blood oath. As soon as Assata was done reciting the oath, Lady Red attempted to snuff her on the right side, but Assata had already peeped her out of her peripheral. Assata threw her right arm up, blocking Lady Red's sucker punch, then immediately threw a left jab followed by a straight right to RedBone's chin, dropping her. Red Bone was out cold. Now all Assata had to worry about was two.

"Work!" Bizzy yelled from the sideline excitedly.

"Get the fuck up!" Assata yelled to Red Bone but had her focus on Black. Lady Red was rushing in for the kill. Black and Assata began to trade punches peppering each other with solid blows while Lady Red worked the side of Assata's head. While trading punches, Assata managed to land a solid straight right to Black's nose facilitating a clean break. Black fell to one knee and held her nose, trying to contain blood loss. Assata quickly spun around while throwing up both arms demonstrating a block used by Joe Frasier knows as the 'Peek-A-Boo.' Lady Red threw a mean combination but nothing penetrated Assata's defense.

Assata used both arms and pushed forward knocking Lady Red off balance, then rushed her with a proficient two-piece that sat her down flat on her ass.

"Time!" Yelled Mama Blood.

"Suwoop! Bdddaattt!" Everybody chanted, loving the way Assata had just put on. Lady Red and Black approached Assata and peaced her up. Welcoming her to the Blood Nation. Mama handed Assata a red flag.

"Welcome home, Blood! You did that shit, yo!" Mama Blood admitted.

Bizzy walked up smiling and handed Assata a blunt. All the Bloods attempted to introduce themselves to Assata, but Bizzy put his arm around her neck and walked her away from them.

"Okay, you nice wit'cha hands, I'ma give you that. That shit was cute and all of that but now, let go put this work in," exclaimed Bizzy.

Chapter 27
DEMONSTRATION IS OUR INITIATION

Bizzy drove down a one-way street known as Quincy Avenue and parked by a Johnny pup. There were foreign cars parked on both sides owned by hustlers, and women everywhere looking to be chose. This one particular hustler stood out from the rest. He was dipped in Christian Louboutin from head to toe and went by the name of Cali. Bizzy's posture denoted anger.

Assata peeps it and takes in all sights and sounds. Cali and Bizzy had smoke that stemmed from Bizzy killing a homie of Cali's. Just recently, Cali had caught Bizzy slipping at a red light, and filled his Porche truck with multiple holes. Bizzy lived miraculously.

"What's poppin, big homie?" Assata implored.

"You view that nigga with that Christian shit on? The one with two bitches in his face?"

"Yeah."

"Flip the clip on that nigga, yo!" Bizzy ordered, voice dripping with maleficent. He handed her a 9mm that had a black frame with a Tungsten Cerakote slide, holding 11 rounds. With no words, Assata clutched the pistol, tucked it in her hoodie and stepped out of the same truck that Cali had riddled with holes. Cali was so enthused with entertaining his fans that he didn't see Bizzy's truck or Assata coming. A few hustlers noticed Assata, admiring her curvaceous frame, her walk, and the way her healthy neatly locked dreads hung from the head of her hoodie. Assata smiled and winked, giving them something to see as she sauntered by.

"Damn shorty!" A hustler enunciated, grabbing his dick.

"Look yo! If I can't fuck you and your friend, ain't nothing happened! Word up!" Cali stated arrogantly.

"How much you paying, trick ass nigga?" Shanice implored.

"Paying?"

BOC!

Assata hit Shanice in the back of the head causing blood splatter to rain out on Cali's face. Shanice's friend and a few more took off running.

"The fuck you?" Cali pronounced, wiping his face. When he opened his eyes, Assata had the settler of all problems staring deep into her eyes.

BOC!

Assata hit Cali between his eyes, dropping him artistically. She then stood over him.

"I can get use to this, Blood Gang shit," she muttered.

BOC! BOC! BOC!

Assata planted three more hot one's in Cali's chest, then walked off calm and normal as if she didn't just body two people. A few hustlers backed up slowly with their hands up, all except the one who had called out to her by the name of Rocko.

"I see you, ma," Rocko satiated impressed. Assata stopped in front of him, grabbed a handful of his dick and gazed at his eyes.

"Under different circumstances, you could get it," Assata admitted, licking her tongue and walking off. She jumped in the whip with Bizzy and they pulled off.

"Ma, that's how you let the song play on a nigga!" Bizzy said, throwing B's up.

Assata followed suit and peaced Bizzy up.

"Demonstrating is our initiation!" Yelled Bizzy excitedly.

***

Assata was on the phone with Mama Blood when another call came in. Bizzy and Mama blood had been feeding Assata literature to make sure she was 'Double R' or 'Real Right'. Mama Blood was a five-star general, and Bizzy was a 'High', two steps up from Mama Blood.

"Mama Blood, I'm politic wit'chu later. I , gotta take this on the other line."

"Aight, bark at me later, Blood," retorted Mama Blood. Assata clicked over to the other caller.

"Hey, mama!"

"Wassup, baby girl?" Ketta replied happily.

"You already know, I'm missing you."

"I miss you too, baby girl.

Assata laughed happy to be hearing from Ketta. "How my youngins doing?" asked Assata, referring to Shooter and Lil Fif God.

"Them lil niggaz is militatnt! You already know I got 'em."

"That's what I love to hear," Assata asserted.

"Listen, you know your birthday comin' up. I was thinking you should come home a few days before. It ain't nothing else in our way. We all good now."

A few moments passed with Assata collecting her thoughts. "Mama, listen. I'm really on something right na that I can't get into over the phone. I won't be making it home for my birthday but I'll be ready before my next one."

"Before your ... before your next one? What'chu mean?" Ketta asked, confused.

"I'ma stay down here for a while, mama. Trust me, I know what I'm doing," Assata assured.

Ketta was exasperated deeply from not liking what sh was hearing, but respected it. "I don't like it, but I trust you have good motives. Yo' youngins gone be salty about this one."

"They'll be aight, ma. Trust me."

"Aight then. I sent you some more money. Call me if you need me."

"Thank you, and I love you, ma."

"Love you more."

Chapter 28
KNOCK IT OFF

One year later

Bizzy and Assata were kicking it on a second floor V.I.P area in club Exit, blowing ZaZa and sipping Remy. Bizzy usually had a few of his blood drops for security, but tonight he just wanted to kick it with Assata. Bizzy had some thorough Red Riders in his lineup, but none of them compared to Assata. She was cold, calculating, and relentless in her approach after only being in New York for a year. Assata had put in more work than any other blood drop under Bizzy. Every plate that Bizzy or the higher ups presented, Assata took it with no questions asked.

"Yo, you gone do great things, ya heard?" Bizzy told Assata who was slowly sipping out a bottle of Remy. Assata nodded in agreement. "You only have been in town for a little bit, and you are already a five-star general! That shit never happens. Yo word! You done took more plates than all my scraps combined! Hell, you done took more plates than me!"

"What can I say? I love to keep my silver wear dirty!" Assata retorted, her face depicting a satanic smirk.

"You a funny mothafucka, yo. Seriously though, if you keep putting that work in, and walking Double R, in the next year or two, you could be the fuckin' Godmother! Word!"

"The Godmother?"

"Word! Ain't nothing bigger. The council already been politicking about'chu, you know. They view you and all that. Shid, I even put in a good word for you too, ma!" Bizzy exclaimed excitedly.

"So, I'ma be running the south and shit?"

"The South? Ma, you gone be running the whole east coast!"

"We dirty dancing then, Blood," Assata pronounced, knowing that it was on.

Bizzy lifted his bottle for a toast. Assata lifted her bottle, displaying the bust-down red-face Rollie Bizzy had purchased for her birthday. "To you, ma, for paintin' the town red!"

"Bang bang, Billy Gang!" added Assata.

"Woooop!" Bizzy and Assata chanted in unison. They took a shot from the bottle. When Bizzy sat his bottle on the table, he noticed a familiar face approaching. Bizzy smirked and rose to his feet. Assata peeped the vibe and stood beside him. He placed the back of his hand on her stomach. "Stand down, ma."

Assata heard him, but she wasn't listening. She hated the fact that she left her banga in the whip. The man who was approaching was one of Bizzy's scraps. They'd had a disagreement that turned volatile, and now it was smoke on sight.

"Fuck is up?" Lil Blood implored, snatching his pistol from his hip and holding it by his side.

"What the fuck you gone do with that, mothafucka!" Bizzy spat.

Lil Blood attempted to raise the pistol, but Bizzy grabbed his wrist with his left hand and started letting off shots through his hoodie, hitting Lil Blood four times in the stomach. Bizzy then used his left hand to push Lil Blood to the ground. Assata immediately followed up by jumping up and down on Lil Blood's head. The crowds dispersed hysterically for the front exit.

"Punk mothafucaka!" Bizzy yelled then pulled Assata by her arm. "Come on!"

"Stupid nigga!" Assata yelled before taking off with Bizzy through the back door.

***

The next morning, Assata awoke to the sound of Jada entering her room. Assata attempted to wipe the sleepiness from her face, then sat up and stretched.

"Morning," Jada greeted, making herself comfortable on Assata's bed.

Assata made note of Jada's appearance. Jada had her hair pressed and layered. It hung past her shoulders and complemented her perfectly shaped face, making her look extremely feminine instead of tomboyish. "What's poppin'?" Assata retorted. "What's with this new look? You've been watchin' Love and Basketball or some shit? Nall, you done found you a nigga?"

Jada laughed at Assata.

"I'm serious! You done got'chu some dick, huh?"

"Fuck no, yo! I love me some pussy. Me and my girl goin' out to Tompkins Park for the Summer Jam. You wanna come, yo?" asked Jada.

"Nah, I'm cool! You looking good though."

"Thank you."

"Bizzy in there?"

"Yeah, he in there fucking Mama," Jada informed nonchalantly.

"And you knew that how?"

"You can hear them in the hallway. Anyway, I'm in my bag wit'chu, ma!"

"Wassup?"

"Ever since you started bangin' and mobbin' with Bizzy, you've been neglecting me, yo! We never kick it, and that shit got me salty. Word!" Jada expressed.

"Look, I hear you, and it is not intentional. I just been on my mastermind type shit lately. Plotting and planning, for real."

"You trying to be the Godmother, huh?"

"You already know. Massive action! If I'ma do something, I ain't gone play wit' it. Hard from the start."

"I understand," Jada assured.

"What's poppin?" Bizzy asserted, walking in the room smoking a blunt.

"Tamu, Damu," Assata replied, meaning 'peace blood'.

"Woop." Bizzy handed Assata the blunt. "Aye, yo', Jada. Let me bark at Assata for a minute."

"I'll talk to you later, Assata, and I heard y'all nasty asses to, yo!" Jada exclaimed, bumping Bizzy on the way out.

"That's how your little ass got here!"

"Whatever!" Jada screamed from down the hall.

"Aye, yo, last night was bananas, right? I hit that nigga like four times."

"Yeah, that shit was lit," voiced Assata, passing the blunt back to Bizzy.

"That nigga still alive. He definitely got a shit bag. I tried to kill that nigga, but I only had four shots in that joint. Word!"

"What that shit was about, though?" Questioned Assata.

"That was one of my Blood Drops. He disrespected me, calling me from a jail phone saying things like, he gonna send me where my brother was, and all that. My brother's dead. All this over a misunderstanding. I couldn't get to him, so I set his baby mother's car on fire. Shit exploded and all that. He got out two days ago, and guess somebody spotted me and called him. Punk mothafucka!"

"We need to pay him a visit as soon as he gets released," advised Assata.

"I got it."

"Aight. I wanted to scream at'chu 'bout something."

"I'm all ears, ma," retorted Bizzy, taking a seat on a bean bag.

"I wanna fly two of my youngins up here, and put 'em on."

"You ain't flew 'em yet? Shid, you know the vibe. Paint the city red!"

"I just wanted to run it by you first, big homie."

"It's all love, yo'. Them lil niggaz 'bout that wiz?

Assata displayed an arrogant smirk. "Rhetorical questions this early in the morning? Knock it off," she replied, grabbing her phone to make a call.

Chapter 29

FUCK IT!

Ketta sat at the bar on US 1 called The Hilltop, with ten shots of Buttery Nipples in front of her. Shooter and Lil Fif God flew out to New York to see Assata, so Ketta was feeling lonely, tipsy, and horny. After downing two shots, Ketta's solitude was broken by an extremely handsome young man who took a seat next to her. She gazed at him without embarrassment. Everything about him was magnetic from his appearance to his suavity, and Ketta was attracted to him.

"Let me get two shots of Patron and two Remy," stated the extremely handsome man.

The sound of his voice stirred something between Ketta's legs. She shifted and bit her bottom lip seductively. "Wassup wit'chu?" Ketta asked, giving him the *I wanna fuck you* look with her nipples visibly hard.

"How you doin', gorgeous?" He retorted, downing a shot of Patron followed by a shot of Remy.

"In all honesty, I'd be better if you took me to your car and put that dick in me. Right here, right now," Ketta pronounced looking him square in the eyes.

He chuckled. "I see you a straight shooter. A man of my caliber can appreciate that, but right na, I'm koolin'." He downed another shot.

"You seeing somebody?" Ketta questioned.

"I'on even know no more."

"You fucking somebody?"

137

"Ain't we all?"

"It's been a while," Ketta admitted, slipping her hand in his sweats. She felt him grow in her hand and was impressed with his package. "You sho you just koolin'?"

He downed his last shot and gazed at Ketta who he found profoundly attractive. "Fuck it!"

CLAP! CLAP! CLAP! CLAP! CLAP! CLAP! CLAP! CLAP! Ketta's ass smacking against his thighs and stomach made the sound of a bongo. She looked behind her with a super arch in her back and watched him put his back into every stroke he delivered.

"Oooowww…yes! Ssss…right there! Ssss…Right the fuck there! Give me that good dick!" Ketta yelled while throwing her fat ass back.

"Ummmhmmm! That's it! Throw that pussy back on this dick! Sss… Sshit! This pussy good!" Ketta's ass was jiggling so perfectly that he had to look up at the roof to keep from coming.

Ketta felt him slowing down. "Don't stop. Keep that dick comin'!" When he stopped, Ketta proceeded to throw her ass back, gripping the bed sheets and biting her bottom lip.

"Ss…Hold up! I'm finna skee—" He moaned.

Ketta quickly turned around and caught everything that shot from his dick. Normally, she would have some type of moral and was picky about whose dick she sucked, but she had so much pressure built up that she was like 'fuck it'. On top of that, she was extremely attracted to him. She sucked him good until it started to tickle.

"Damn, ma!" He moaned. Her moaning while giving him head aroused him again.

Ketta pushed him, forcing him to lay back on his back. She mounted him, placed her hands on his chest and began to bounce on his dick aggressively. He grabbed both of her ass cheeks and moved with her to a chaotic rhythm. After she came twice, she slowed her pace and rhythm that was equated to making love. He caressed the deep arch in her back and sucked both of her nipples while she slow fucked him passionately.

"You feel so fucking good inside this pussy," Ketta moaned. "I want'chu to nut in me. Sss...Ssshit! Cum for me, daddy!"

"F-Fuck! I'm skeeting in this pussy!"

Ketta leaned down and tongue kissed him while bouncing on his dick until she felt his warm semen shoot deep in her. He came and continued to kiss her passionately. They were in a state of bliss and couldn't believe how good they felt to each other.

"Yo' dick fits perfectly in my pussy, like it was made for it," Ketta remarked, leaning in kissing him again.

"For real. That pussy was everything," he retorted, flipping her over. He kissed her on the lips then made her turnover on her stomach.

"I don't know what this is, but I do know I want this shit in my life," he whispered in her ear, kissed it, and sucked on it.

"Ummm!" Ketta moaned.

He placed a kiss on her neck, on both shoulders, then made a trail down her back. Ketta arched her back, moaning seductively. He made his way down the crack of her ass with his tongue, blew softly then placed kisses on both cheeks, sending chills through Ketta's entire body. He made his way down the back of her thighs and kissed on the back of her knees.

"Ssss...oooowww!" she cried.

After sucking on the heel of her feet, he made his way back up to her ass cheeks, then guided her to lay face down, ass up position. He spread her ass cheeks, slipped his tongue in and out of her ass then slipped his thumb in her asshole.

"Oh-My-God!"

He moved his thumb in and out of her ass and began to suck her pussy from the back, driving Ketta bananas.

"Aaaahhh! FFuck! Ssss... SShit yes! Ssss...Whooo-baby!" Ketta cried out as he made her cum simultaneously in her ass and pussy. Ketta collapsed on the bed and began to tremble. When her trembling subsided, he entered her gently and began to slow stroke her from behind, long and deep. Ketta was so wet that you could hear her pussy smacking with each stroke. This total stranger was fucking her so good that she clutched her pillow and cried tears of pleasure. No man had ever made her cry during sex. Ketta was in a dubious state of mind.

***

"Yo, I see you've been living up to your name. Word, homie!" Proclaimed Frank who was a barber and owner of a barber shop on Nostrand Avenue.

"You already know demonstration is my initiation," Bizzy philosophized while sitting in the barber chair getting a line up.

Frank always looked forward to Bizzy coming to the shop. He knew that he was guaranteed a good laugh. Bizzy was a vicious serial killer but was also a funny mothafucka with a good heart.

"Aye yo, you remember when we were on the island, and I had to stop you from cutting mothafuckas! You had like three days before going home, yo," Frank reminisced.

"Yo, I swear on my mother! I was gone butcher them niggas, lick the scalpel and catch hepatitis C around this mothafucka! Word!" added Bizzy.

Frank and everybody else in the shop got a good laugh out of Bizzy. "You a funny nigga, forreal yo." Frank leaned in and whispered in Bizzy's ear, "Yo, I need you to hit me off with two of the joints, B," Frank said referring to two bricks of Fetty.

"I got'chu, son," assured Bizzy.

Frank brushed the hair out of Bizzy's face and removed the cloak from around his neck.

"Yo' I'm sending my lil mans to the spot with that, you heard?" Bizzy implored, standing from the chair.

"Word!" Frank replied.

On his way out, Bizzy spotted someone he knew. "What's poppin', homie?"

"Yo, what up, big homie?" The man by the name of Blaze retorted sitting next to his girlfriend.

"I view you with that shit on," Bizzy acknowledged, referring to the jewels Blaze and his girlfriend were draped in.

"Yeah, you already know yo'."

"Stay up, homie," Bizzy stated before walking out of the shop. Bizzy hopped in his truck and fired up a blunt of Za.

Blaze rose to sit in the barber chair, but Frank stopped him. "Hold up. You next, yo'. I got one more ahead of you."

"Yo, this is some bullshit, homie. I been here for an hour, yo," cried Blaze.

"You next, homie."

Blaze sucked his teeth. "What I gotta do, pay VIP?"

"None of that, homie. I'm loyal to my customers. You next, homie."

The shop door opened, and two masked men rushed in. *BOC! BOC! BOC!* Three shots hit Blaze in the head, face and neck, dropping him rigorously.

BOC! BOC! BOC! BOC! Four shots ripped through Blaze's girlfriend's face and chest, dropping her next to her lover. The two gunmen grabbed the jewelry from the dead bodies and rushed out the way they came in. They hopped in the truck with Bizzy and Assata then slid off.

"Yo, that shit was impeccable! You lil niggas is like that! Word!" Bizzy announced excitedly, passing the blunt to Lil Fif God.

"All in a day's work," retorted Shooter.

Assata sat in silence with a smile on her face.

"I like you lil niggaz! Word!" Bizzy had fronted Blaze a brick of Fetty and he failed to clean his face. It inflamed Bizzy to see Blaze and his girl draped in jewels knowing he was owed money. Shooter and Lil Fif God's initiation was putting Blaze under. His girlfriend was just collateral damage. "You niggas keep them jewels, ya heard? Welcome to the Billy Gang, homiez!" Bizzy hit the joint, inhaled deeply, then exhaled. "That's how you let the song play on a mothafucka!"

Chapter 30
BILLY GET'EM, BILLY GOT'EM!

Three Days Later…

Shooter and Lil Fif God were on flight back to Florida while Bizzy and Assata stood out in front of Fort Green Projects, smoking blunts and politicking gang life.

"You got a few drops up under you from New York, and that is kool and all that. Now, you gotta go back to your city and paint that mothafucka red, ya heard?" Bizzy politicked, moving his hands around all animated like.

"I hear you," Assata replied.

"Yo, and then you gotta paint the whole fucking state of Florida red and move your way back up! Billies everywhere around this mothafucka!"

"Always and forever!" Assata added.

"Black Wall Street!"

"Revolutionary reflection!"

"Woooppp!" Bizzy and Assata chatted in unison, throwing up Big Bs. Moments later, a red 2020 Range Rover sports edition pulled up and a young, rich nigga named YB hopped out, designer down, dripping in jewels.

"Wass poppin'?" YB greeted Bizzy, bumping Bs together.

"You already know this five," Bizzy pronounced. "Yo, this who I was telling you about. Assata. Assata, this my manz, YB."

"Wass popping, ma?" YB implored, throwing up the B to peace up Assata but Assata just looked at him and lifted her head up.

It was something about him that Assata wasn't feeling. "Wass popping?" Assata responded dryly.

"Yo, ma, he homie. Peace him up," Bizzy encouraged.

YB never been through the flame or put no real work in to be homie. He paid his way in instead. YB was originally introduced to the 9 Trey Gangsta Bloods through another member, but once he saw how vicious Bizzy's murder game was, he kept him under his wing with an endless supply of Fetty, money, and jewelry. This angered a homie by the name of Snow.

Assata peaced YB up ambivalently.

"I hear good things about'chu, ma," YB exclaimed.

"My name is Assata."

"My fault, yo. Assata. My man vouches for you. Anything you need— *anything*— say word, and it's down," YB assured.

"That's wassup," retorted Assata, not impressed.

"Aye, yo, let me scream at'chu for a minute over here," YB told Bizzy.

"Pardon me, homie," Bizzy told Assata, then sat in the truck with YB. "Wassup, homie?"

"We got a problem."

"Talk to me. Wassup?"

YB pulled out his phone. "My mans sent me this two days ago." YB played the recording.

Lil Manz: "Yo, I don't hear you. What'chu said?"

Snow: "I said I'ma rob that nigga YB and kill that nigga Bizzy!"

Lil Manz: "For what, yo? Both of them is good niggaz! YB and Bizzy be looking out for you, yo! Yo, you buggin' for real, homie. Word!"

Snow: "Yo, fuck all that! I'ma kidnap that bitch azz nigga YB, just like we did 69, and I'm killin' Bizzy! That's my word, homie!"

Bizzy's face was screwed up while his blood was boiling. "Yo, yo' manz sent this two days ago, right?"

"Yeah."

"Yo, homie! You supposed to let me hear that two days ago! Niggaz could've got the drop on me, homie!" Bizzy spat seethingly.

"I was out of town, yo. I wanted to let'chu hear it in person," explained YB.

Bizzy exhaled then lit a Newport. "Yo, don't trip. I'ma handle it."

"Hit me when it's done, yo. I'm out," YB stated.

"Alright, homie," retorted Bizzy, peacing up YB before hopping out of the truck.

When YB pulled off, Assata, always paying attention to detail, noticed a shift in Bizzy's energy. "You good, big homie?"

"Yeah, I'm bool," retorted Bizzy, flicking the cigarette butt to the pavement. He then pulled a Backwood from behind his ear and handed it to Assata. "Light up, homie."

Assata lit the leaf, then noticed two niggas approaching behind Bizzy. "Watch yo' bix, homie," Assata warned, sliding her right hand in the hoodie, clutching her bliky while smoking the leaf with her left. Bizzy swiveled, clutching his pistol.

"Be easy, yo! It's me," declared the approaching man and his compadre.

"Wass poppin', homie," Bizzy implored, throwing Bs up.

"Five alive! You know what it is."

Bizzy loosened up, but Assata continued to clutch her pistol. "Be easy, shorty. Don't hurt nobody out were today." Assata remained silent. "What's the word, homie?" Bizzy questioned reaching for the blunt.

"Me and my manz need to ride over to Marcy's."

"Hop in, yo. Assata let's roll out." Bizzy hopped in the driver's seat while Assata jumped in the back.

When they arrived at Marcy's Projects, Bizzy hopped out and made a phone call. The two men hopped out, while Assata remained in the backseat.

"Aye, yo, Bizzy! Let me bark at'chu for a minute, homie."

"Yo, hold on!" Bizzy retorted with the phone to his ear, surveying his surroundings.

BOC!

Bizzy drew his 9-millimeter swiftly and hit Snow in the back of his head, dropping him. He then turned to Snow's man, but he knocked Bizzy's hand down and took off running. By this time, Assata had hopped out and started busting shots at the unknown man.

BOC! BOC! BOC! BOC! BOC! BOC!

Bizzy and Assata attempted to follow Snow's man, but he was too fast. Bizzy looked down at Snow and saw that he was dead. He then hopped back in the truck and pulled off.

"What the fuck, my nigga?" Assata questioned perplexed.

"Remember my man, YB? The one who pulled up in the Rover?"

"What about 'em?"

"When I hopped in the whip wit' 'em, he let me hear a recording of that nigga Snow saying certain shit like he gone kill me and rob my mans."

"I'm assuming, Snow is the nigga back there on the ground.

"Yeah," Bizzy declared, lighting a cigarette.

"Who the other nigga was?"

"I'on know, homie. He came wit' 'em, so I was gonna put him down wit' 'em."

"I overstand," Assata assured.

"Yo, that nigga was fast as shit! Word!"

Assata and Bizzy shared a good laugh.

"Good lookin', too, homie."

"You, know the vibe! Billy get'em, Billy got'em!"

"You know Billy Shot 'em!" Bizzy added.

"Woopp!" They both chanted in unison, bumping Big Bs together.

Chapter 31
THE LINE UP

After grabbing hot dogs and pizza, Arlicia drove down Monroe Avenue and pulled in front of her brownstone with Jada and Assata in the car with her.

"What the two of you about to do?" Arlicia asked.

"Jada always cryin' that we never kick it, so I guess we finna watch something on the Fire Stick," Assata asserted.

"You, really don't be kickin' it with me, yo!" Jada added.

Arlicia's phone rang.

"Hello?" She answered. "Okay, hold on for a minute. Aye, y'all get out. I gotta handle some business."

Jada and Assata grabbed their food, then headed inside.

Arlicia pulled off and continued her conversation.

"Okay, what do you need me to do?"

"Look, I need you to go pick a package up in Midtown, then take it to 34th," explained YB.

"Yo', why you ain't called Bizzy?" Arlicia questioned.

"I did yo', but he ain't picking up. Come on ma, I need you!" YB pleaded. Arlicia pondered her decision.

"When you drop the pack off, it should be 50 grand. You keep ten, and bring me 40. My mans is in midtown waiting with the pack."

"Okay, I'll do it," she stated.

"Aight Shorty. Look for a white Audi truck," YB instructed.

"I got it, yo'," she assured. Click! Arlicia hung the phone up and headed to midtown.

"Bizzy gone kill me if he find out," Arlicia said out loud to herself. Once she received the package from YB's mans, she headed over to 34th.

"Where the fuck is this nigga at yo'?" Arlicia questioned pulling her phone out to call YB.

"Wassup shorty?" answered YB.

"Yo', I'm on 34th and your mans ain't here. I'on see no white Audi, yo'!"

"He, just hit me ma. He around the corner." Click!

"Hello? Yo', YB!" YB had hung up the phone.

"This motha fucka, yo!" cried Arlicia as she crept at a low speed looking for the white Audi. Scrrrrrrrrrrrr!!!!

Out of nowhere, unmarked vehicles surrounded Arlicia's X6 M Series.

Masked men hopped out with rifles barking orders for her to step out with her hands up. almost defecating on herself, Arlicia realized at that moment, she'd been set up. she stepped out of her vehicle and surrendered peacefully.

***

"Aye, yo', hand me that bottle out of the icebox homie," YB asked Bizzy. Bizzy opened the glove box and grabbed the bottle of 1738 from the icebox.

"Icebox?" Assata questioned. "You gotta icebox in the glove box?" YB chuckled.

"Everything's presidential over here, Shorty," Boasted YB.

"You wanna taste?" Bizzy offered.

"I'm bool, homie," Assata retorted, relaxing in the butter soft interior while enjoying the scenery. Bizzy was on the run for the shooting in club Exit, so YB insisted on taking a trip to PA. They were on Interstate 78 headed to the casino to relax and gamble.

"You wanna hit this gas yo'?" Bizzy asked Assata, handing her a blunt.

"Yea," she replied, grabbing the blunt and tracking a toke. As soon as Assata blew smoke from her nose, the truck lit up with red and blue lights.

"Fuck yo'! Roscoe behind us," Bizzy exclaimed referring to the cops.

"Relax, yo'. Just, put the blunt out," YB advised pulling over. Assata hit the blunt once more before putting it out.

"Yo', I got all kinds of shit on me, son. Why the fuck is you pullin' over?" Bizzy implored annoyed.

"Relax homie," retorted YB.

"Relax?"

"Give me the shit," Assata told Bizzy. Bizzy gave Assata a dubious look.

"Tightin' up homie," Assata pronounced. Bizzy handed Assata four ounces of fetty and a pistol. She tucked it in her hoodie and relaxed. Moments later, a trooper approached YB's side with a flashlight.

"What seems to be the problem, officer?" Questioned YB.

"Wooo! Smells good in here, boy! License and registration!" Barked the trooper. YB grabbed his information and handed it to the trooper.

"What's your name, boy?" The trooper asked Bizzy, shining the flashlight in his face. Bizzy started to give him a alias but said fuck it.

"Aaron Young," Bizzy pronounced.

"You in the back, there?"

"Assata Moss! The trooper headed to his cruiser to run the information while doing this another trooper pulled up to assist.

"Yo', I gotta warrant son. They about to book me. I don't know why you even stopped, yo'," exclaimed Bizzy.

"Relax yo', we all good," YB assured. Assata remained silent awaiting to see how things played out. Once YB noted the trooper and his fellow officer approaching, he pulled out his phone and dialed a number. The trooper handed YB his information.

"Aaron Young! Step outta the -" Before the trooper could finish his demand, YB handed him his phone.

"The hell you handing me a phone for?" The trooper question but still took the phone out of curiosity.

"Yeah?" answered the trooper. Moments later the trooper walked off with the phone.

"Your free to go! Let's go trooper," The trooper told the other trooper who had pulled up to assist. YB put the car in gear, grabbed his bottle of Remy and pulled off as if nothing happened. Assata was burning a whole in the back of Bizzy's head, but he never turned around. Assata knew that Bizzy had just found out that his man's YB was working for the Fedz. Bizzy had a warrant and they still let him go. she came up with the conclusion that Bizzy was just elated that he made it out that situation ... for now!

Chapter 32
YOU'VE BEEN BAD AGAIN

Assata tried to call G.I. for the fourth time, only to receive the voicemails. She hadn't spoken to him in a week's time and was missing him dearly. The long-distance relations were strenuously difficult, and Assata was becoming home sick. After leaving the casino, Assata laid low with Bizzy in Brevolt Projects on Howard Avenue, building 260. This spot was one of Bizzy's duck off spots and was only used when necessary. Assata made her way into a living room where Bizzy sat on the couch smoking a blunt.

"Wass poppin'?" Bizzy greeted Assata.

"Wassup, big homie?" Assata retorted, bumping Bs with Bizzy. He offered the blunt to her, but she declined. "What that B 'bout, last night?" Assata questioned.

"What'chu mean?"

"Wassup wit'cha mans and that trooper?"

"Yo', I'on know what that was about. That shit threw me off, but I was just glad that we rolled the fuck up outta there. Word!" Bizzy hit that blunt and blew smoke from his nose.

"I had my banga on me, so I was glad we made it out, but yo' nigga workin'!" Assata voiced.

"What'chu mean?"

"That nigga, YB the fucking police! He a rat, nigga!" Assata expressed laconically.

"You think so, yo'"? Assata just looked at Bizzy like he was crazy.

152

"Nall yo'. I'on think so, homie," Bizzy exclaimed. YB gave Bizzy anything he wanted. There was never a time that YB told him no, and Bizzy never told him no when he needed a body dropped. Bizzy was protecting his walking ATM by any means.

"I view you in denial. Just keep that nigga from 'round me. I hate rats!"

"That shit was weird, yo, but i'on know, ya heard." Bizzy got an alert letting him know that he had a text message. The messages came from one of his lil homies named X and it was pictures of unmarked cars.

"The fuck is this shit?" Bizzy implored. Moments later his phone rang.

"Yo!"

"You got my message, homie?" X questioned.

'Yeah, what is that?"

"Yo, big homie! The FEDS got the whole building surrounded, homie!"

"Aye yo, good looking out homie."

Click!

"Damn! Fuck you gone do, homie?" Assata asked.

"Yo, hold on," Bizzy retorted, getting up to peek out of the window.

"Damn yo! These mothafuckas are really out there." Bizzy took a picture of the FEDS then sent it to YB. After sending the picture, moments later a few Federal Task Force members looked right at the window Bizzy was in.

"Oh shit!" Bizzy quickly shut the curtain and jumped back from the window. "Them mothafuckas just looked right up here yo!"

"What the fuck? Who you sent that picture to?" Assata questioned.

"YB!"

"I told you that bitch ass nigga working!" Spat Assata seethingly.

"Aye, do me a favor yo'."

"Wassup?" Bizzy went in his pocket and handed Assata fifty dollars.

"Go to the store and grab me some backwoods yo. Hit me, and let me know what they doing," Assata dressed quickly and grabbed her pistol.

"Nall yo'. Leave that in here in case they grab you, homie." Assata handed Bizzy the pistol.

"Aye yo', you know it's all love homie." Bizzy bumped Bs with Assata, then hugged her tight.

"I love you, homie," Bizzy stated.

"Love you too, big homie," Assata retorted then headed out the door. Bizzy locked it, headed to the bathroom, got in the tub and closed the shower curtain. He waited a minute to see if Assata would call, but she never did. The FEDS snatched her and moved her away from the building. Bizzy then called his six-year-old daughter Brooklyn on Facetime.

"Hey, baby girl," Bizzy whispered.

"Daddy, why are you whispering in the dark?"

"Listen, something is going down. If you don't hear from me, I'm in jail."

"You've been bad again daddy?" Brooklyn asked in the sweetest voice.

"Yes, baby girl. I'm sorry and I love you, okay?"

"I love you too, daddy!" Bizzy heard the front door being kicked in.

"I gotta go, baby girl!"

Click!

Bizzy heard them enter the room.

"I'm in here, yo! Don't shoot! Don't shoot, I'm in here!" Yelled Bizzy. One of the task force members snatched the shower curtain back.

"Get on the fucking ground!"

154

Chapter 33
SOLID, LOYAL

On a plane back to Florida, Assata gazed out of the window pensively. She thought about how the agents had grabbed her when she stepped out of Bizzy's duck off apartment. Assata thought that she was being detained, but they only were cleaning the building before taking Bizzy down. He was labeled armed and dangerous, so moving Assata was only a precaution. Assata stayed with Jada two more days before booking a flight back home. It was then, she learned that Bizzy had been caught up in a big indictment with the 9 Trey Gangsta Bloods. She was made aware that YB had set Jada's mother up and gave up Bizzy's location. Snow had survived and cooperated while Six Nine didn't make it any better. Assata thought of how highly Bizzy spoke of YB, and all the work he'd put in for him, all to find out that his loyalty was his downfall. All the work Assata had put in, she was elated that she missed the indictment.

Back in Fort Pierce, Assata's first stop was to Ketta's. She knocked on the door and waited patiently. Moments later Ketta opened the door smiling infectiously.

"Damn mom, is that smile for me, or the sex slave you got trapped in there somewhere?" Assata asked, smiling back herself.

"What makes you think. I got somebody in here?" Ketta retorted, grabbing Assata pulling her close and planting a kiss on her cheek.

"Mama look at wat'chu got on! Plus, you smell like CoCo Mademoiselle, and sex."

Ketta laughed. "Okay, damn! I do gotta lil snack back there. I'ma let'chu meet'em later. But, on some other shit, I'm so fucking happy you back, baby. I love you and missed you something, terrible."

"I love you too, mama," Assata expressed hugging Ketta again.

"Why you ain't tell me you were coming back? I would of picked you up and had a party planned.

"Wanted to surprise you."

"Well, I'm surprised like a mothafucka. I'm glad you're back, but this is where I ask you to come back later, so I can finish working my sex slave," Ketta pronounced chuckling.

"Okay mama. I'll call you later. Love You." Assata stated before kissing Ketta on the cheek and turning to leave.

***

Assata had called Wolly and told him that she was on the way. He cleared the store and waited for her arrival. When Assata pulled up, she found Wolly leaning on his 2022 850 HP GMC Sierra Sports Edition in an all-white linen suit smoking a cigar. Assata hopped out of the Yenko truck in a pair of all Red Palm Angels track pants, a tank top, a pair of red Bally champion sneakers, and her dreads were now all red.

"Assata! How are you, my friend?" Wolly asked in his deep Arabian accent.

"Wassup, Wolly? I'm just cooling," retorted Assata, hugging Wolly.

"Who?"

"I'm alright, Wolly," Said Assata, smiling.

"I'm happy you're here. Come!" Wolly headed to the door and held it open for Assata. He then locked it and headed to his secret hidden room. Wolly grabbed a bottle of Blonde rum and poured two shots.

"For you," Wolly declared, handing Assata a shot glass.

"Thank you," she replied downing the shot.

"Listen, my friend. I don't want to sugar coat. What are your plans?

"I'm finna get this money, Wolly," Assata stated firmly.

"I thought so," he admitted, pouring two more shots. "To riches! Salute!"

"To riches!" Assata announced then downed her shot.

"Wolly, I appreciate it, but it's one more thing I need you to help me with," she explained.

"For you my friend, anything! Name it."

***

"Listen! I gotta go handle some shit, I'll be back in a few days. I want'chu niggaz to hold shit down on Ave S while I'm gone. Overstood?" Assata implored.

"Yeah, we got'chu, Queen," Lil Fif God assured.

"You know we gone hold it down. Been holding it down," Shooter added.

"I know y'all be proving y'all loyalty, and this is why I wanted y'all to know that I'm given y'all the third floor."

"What you mean, Queen?" Shooter questioned.

"Both of y'all arc three star generals. I trust yall's judgment, so start breeding dogs! We gone, paint the city and the whole Florida red!"

"Wooopp!" Lil Fif God chanted.

"Always and Foreva!" Shooter added.

"I love you lil niggas," Exclaimed Assata, peacing both of them up.

"We love you more, Queen!" Shooter reassured.

"Come back here," Assata ordered heading into the room. They followed behind her. When they entered the room. It was a bale of weed on the floor, 10 bricks of fetty, and 10 bricks of coke.

"Y'all view this shit? This shit here is life changing type shit. We taking over the whole tri-county. All y'all gotta do is remain solid...loyal!"

"Knock it off, Queen. You already know the vibe," Shooter asserted.

Chapter 34
BIDNESS

G.I. entered Assata's apartment and locked the door behind him. It had been a little over a year since he'd been with Assata in the physical, so the anticipation was an overload. Assata had called him, and told him to come over, and the door would be opened.

"Mmm...Hmmm! Sss...yes!" The moans of Assata could be heard coming from her room.

"Damn," G.I. whispered, grabbing his dick as he entered her room. When he entered the room, Assata had her left leg behind her head while using her right hand to push a 9 inch dildo in and out of her drenched pussy. Once she locked eyes with G.I., she removed the dildo, placed half of it in her mouth and sucked her nectar from it.

"Sshit!" Moaned G.I. removing all articles of clothing. He jumped in the bed and dove headfirst into Assata's love nest. G.I stuck his entire tongue in and out of her pussy just to get a taste of the juices, then focused his attention on her clit.

"Mmmm," Assata moaned while making slurping sounds. She held G.I.'s dreads in her left hand and rolled her hips while continuing to suck on the dildo. G.I. was so turned on that he had an abundance of pre-cum oozing from his dick. Once he felt Assata cuming in his mouth, he crawled up her body leaving a trail of kisses behind. He grabbed the dildo from her hand, threw it aside and began kissing her passionately. Assata's body reciprocated as she grabbed G.I.'s dick and guided him to another world.

"Fffuck," G.I. whispered in her ear as he slid deep into her love canal.

"I know," Assata whispered back in his ear, then began to suck on it and claw into his back as he moved in and out of her artistically. Assata's arrogance turned G.I. on, forcing him to cum early. He picked up his pace, stroking deep and abstrusely prompting Assata to cum with him.

"Ssss....Ooowhooo, Ffffuck, daddy!" She cried as her pussy became abnormally wet. The sound of friction echoed through the apartment creating a familiar symphony. Assata's pussy was so amazing that G.I didn't get soft. He rose up and admired the way Assata's labium grabbed at his dick when he stroked in and out of her. Assata's pussy was so pretty that G.I. had to snatch it out of her and eat it. He latched on her clit and pushed two fingers up in her hitting her G-Spot.

"Yes! SSS...NNNN....HMMMM! Eat this pussy!" yelled Assata as she came in his mouth.

"Mmmm," G.I. moaned, swallowing all that dripped. Assata flipped over and proceeded to ride G.I.'s face.

"Stick that tongue out, daddy," she demanded. G.I. did as he was told. Assata bit her bottom lip and looked back at her own ass while she twerked on his tongue. She came again instantly. G.I. smacked both of her ass cheeks.

"Sss. Aaah!" Cried Assata squeezing her pussy muscle and grinding hard on G.I.'s face. She then slid down his face to mount his throbbing dick. The moment she wiggled down on G.I. dick, he moaned in pure bliss. Her pussy was so warm and wet.

"I fuckin' love you!" G.I. cried as Assata bounced up and down on his dick poetically.

"Love you too, nigga! Ssshit!" Assata yelled, cuming again. Assata's pussy juice splashed about as she leaned down and sucked G.I.'s nipple while continuing to ride him. This method had G.I. conflicted.

"Sss...Shit!" G.I. yelled as he came deep off in Assata.

"I feel you, daddy," Assata expressed as his warm semen shot deep inside of her.

"Mmmm..." Assata moaned while kissing him passionately and grinding on him until all was empty in him. G.I. massaged her ass cheeks and sucked on one of her nipples briefly.

"I missed you, Africa," Assata voice calling G.I. by the nickname she gave him.

"I've missed you more, dimples," he retorted, gazing into her enchanting eyes. Assata kissed him, unmounted him, then laid beside him and rubbed his chest. Moments later, Assata noticed that G.I. was staring at the roof, and appeared to be in deep thought.

"Wassup, bae?" Assata asked, still caressing his chiseled chest. He snapped out of his trance.

"Nothing bae. It's just that, it's been a while. A nigga missed you, like really though."

"Awwl, come on na. You tougher than that. We both know I had to leave for a while. I gotta lot of shit handled when I was in New York."

"Like what?" Questioned G.I.

"I'll put'chu on game later," Assata promised.

G.I. seemed slightly disappointed.

"Yeah, I hear you," he satiated dryly.

"It's something else I gotta tell you, though," she said sitting up to look him in his eyes.

"Wassup, Assata?"

"I gotta leave town again for like two weeks."

"For what?"

"Bidness," she retorted sternly.

Chapter 35
A LONG STORY

Allah hu Akber Allah Hu Akbar
Allah hu Akbar Allah ho Akbar
Ash-hadu- on-la ha-illallah
Ash-hadu- on-la ha-illallah

Nara, the muezzin and also Khafre's wife began to recite the call for prayer that stated. "God is great, God is great." "I bear witness that there is no god but God." After his pilgrimage to Egypt, Khafre hid in a village in Eritrea, a place in Africa north of Ethiopia. He'd taken a wife from Sudan and had become a devout Muslim. When the time was appropriate, he had planned to send for Ketta to be another wife to him, and for Assata and Hassan to join him in Africa, but the time had yet to come. He washed up at a nearby stream to get ready for prayer, when he noticed a beautiful woman next to him doing the same. She was eloquently wrapped in a garment that covered her hair and had beads around her wrist. She also wore golden rings on each finger, and one in her nose. Khafre had never seen her in the village before, but she looked familiar.

"Salaam, aleikum," Khafre greeted, meaning 'peace be with you.' The beautiful young woman lifted her face from the steam to face Khafre. His eyes grew wide as recognition set in.

"Wa alaikum Salaam," Assata retorted, drawing a primitive AK from underneath her garment and Swiss cheesing her father. Khafre fell into the stream, his blood puddling around him as the current carried his body onward.

"Tell my brothers I sent'chu, mothafucka!" Yelled Assata.

"Assata!" Yelled Patty in confusion who stood next to her son, Baby G. Assata was taken aback to see her great grandmother standing next to her grandfather?

Tears began to fall freely from her face as she admired how beautifully both of them had aged.

"Why did you do it? Why?" Patty screams hysterically. Assata exhaled deeply then raised the AK.

"It's a long story, grandma."

KATKATKATKATKTA!

***

When Assata came back to the city, Lil Fif God and Shooter had already bred three more drops by the names of Red Face, Lil Soulja, and Heman. They were all at Assata's house on Avenue S in the garage getting ready to go put work in. Fif God and Shooter had sent them through the flames, but Assata wanted to see what their gun game was hitting on. She had given them all potent X-pills to use for influence. Once she seen the pills taking affect, she moved in with a calculated tactic.

"We finna go kill these niggaz, and take over the city," she chanted in each one of their ears, while massaging their shoulders. They gritted their teeth, inhaled, exhaled blissfully enjoying a euphoric high while clutching their weapons.

"We still here?" Questioned Lil Soulja ready to put pain in.

"That's what the fuck I'm talking about. Let's slide!" Assata ordered.

Assata hopped in a Toyota truck, while her drops jumped in a Kia truck and followed behind her. When she pulled up on 14th Street, the Avenue was chocked with hustlers, killers, and women looking to be chosen. Assata hopped out with a Draco in hand, while her youngins did the same.

DOOM! DOOM! DOOM!

Assata let the Draco loose in the air causing a terrifying silence to tear through the atmosphere. Her youngins stood on guard holding assault rifles, itching to kill.

"Listen up!" Assata spoke up, walking back and forth holding the baby Draco in the air like an umbrella. Ain't no more trappin' over here, unless you bloody steppin'! All transgressions will be dealt with accordingly. I am Assata, and I approve of this message!" Red Face, Lil Soulja, and Heman all hit the kill switch on their rifles and waved them from side to side dropping bodies boisterously. Shooter and Lil Fif God followed suit standing over bodies and filling them with hot shit. Assata hit a few people with the Draco, then hopped back in the truck.

"Suwoop!" Sung Assata grabbing the young killas' attention. They hopped back in the Kia and snatched off behind Assata. She admired their bestiality as she headed to every other territory worth taking over and did the same. In a short time, Assata had painted the whole city red, and took over all territories. If you weren't banging Blood, you had to remain neutral or die. Assata was making so much noise that she was getting calls from the higher ups on a regular basis. She was a whole different type of force to be reckoned with.

Chapter 36
THE COUNCIL

Assata was lying in bed comfortably with G.I. loving on her, when her phone rang.

"Yeah?" She answered.

"Wass popping yo?" Asked Bizzy.

Assata laughed happy to be hearing from the big homie.

"You already know, us neva them!"

Bizzy had signed a plea for twenty years to the RICO act, and the attempted murder of Snow. The club shooting was scrapped do to recantation from the victim. Bizzy was now calling from a cell phone in Big Sandy.

"You know the vibe! Aye yo, view this though, homie. I got the council on line with me, and they wanna bark at'chu you heard?" Informed Bizzy. The council are the Godfathers from each set under the U.B.N. United Blood Nation.

"Twenty-one- hunnid!" retorted Assata.

"What's popping?" Each member of the council greeted and induced themselves.

"Woooop!" said Assata.

"Listen, we ain't gonna take up too much of your time. You've been under review for a little over two years now, and we recognize your abilities to lead in the nation. Never in the history of banging has a woman gained stain so quickly and breed as many as you have. We, the council have voted, and all are in favor of crowning you. "The Blood Godmother!"

"To the council, I accept, and I'm honored to be a part of this almighty structure!" Added Assata.

"Congratulations, homie! Cheered Bizzy.

"Thanks, big homie!

"I'm not your big homie no more, baby girl. You got mo' stain than me now!" Bizzy asserted with laughter.

"You gon' always be the big homie," Assata said sincerely.

"I hear that but peep though. I'ma get at'chu later, homie," Bizzy stated.

"Aight. You know it's all love," assured Assata.

"Always and forever, yo'! Word!"

"Stay 0-50!"

Click!

"Who was that, bae?" Questioned G.I.

"Just one of the homies," Assata told him.

"Everything aight?"

"Yeah, daddy," said Assata, leaning in to kiss G.I. and mount him. As soon as he grabbed his dick to insert in her, there was a knock at the door.

"Hold that though, bae," exclaimed Assata kissing him before getting up to answer the door. She peeked out of the curtain, and saw that it was her mother, Ketta. Assata smiled and opened the door.

"Heeyy, mama!"

"Wassup, baby girl?" Ketta replied, hugging and kissing Assata on the cheek.

"What blew you over here?"

"I wanted to tell you something, but I wanted to tell you in person," Ketta stated happily.

"Wassup, mama?" she asked curiously. Ketta rubbed her stomach before replying.

"I'm pregnant!" She revealed excitedly.

"Mama. That's some brazy shit!" Assata mentioned smiling.

"Why you say that?"

166

"Kuz I was gone tell you the same shit when I saw you, but'chu here na. I can't believe this shit, ma!"

"Well, shid, when you gone let me meet my son-in-law?" Ketta questioned.

"He's here, mama. Bae! Bae, come here for a minute!" Yelled Assata.

Moments later, G.I. emerged from the back room. Perplexity and fear fan throughout his entire body as the recognition of Ketta set in.

"Mama, this is who I have been seeing for the past three years. This is G.I., the father of my child."

Ketta remained silent as tears of pain fell from the wells of her eyes rapidly.

"What's wrong, mama?" Assata questioned, concerned.

Ketta shook her head then extended her hand. "Nice to meet'chu, G.I," Ketta stated in a whisper.

TO BE CONTINUED ….

Lock Down Publications and Ca$h Presents
Assisted Publishing Packages

BASIC PACKAGE	UPGRADED PACKAGE
$499	$800
Editing	Typing
Cover Design	Editing
Formatting	Cover Design
	Formatting
ADVANCE PACKAGE	**LDP SUPREME PACKAGE**
$1,200	$1,500
Typing	Typing
Editing	Editing
Cover Design	Cover Design
Formatting	Formatting
Copyright registration	Copyright registration
Proofreading	Proofreading
Upload book to Amazon	Set up Amazon account
	Upload book to Amazon
	Advertise on LDP, Amazon and Facebook Page

***Other services available upon request.
Additional charges may apply

Lock Down Publications
P.O. Box 944
Stockbridge, GA 30281-9998
Phone: 470 303-9761

Submission Guideline

Submit the first three chapters of your completed manuscript to ldpsubmissions@gmail.com. In the subject line add **Your Book's Title**. The manuscript must be in a Word Doc file and sent as an attachment. Document should be in Times New Roman, double spaced, and in size 12 font. Also, provide your synopsis and full contact information. If sending multiple submissions, they must each be in a separate email.

Have a story but no way to send it electronically? You can still submit to LDP/Ca$h Presents. Send in the first three chapters, written or typed, of your completed manuscript to:

LDP: Submissions Dept
P.O. Box 944
Stockbridge, GA 30281-9998

DO NOT send original manuscript. Must be a duplicate.
Provide your synopsis and a cover letter containing your full contact information.

Thanks for considering LDP and Ca$h Presents.

NEW RELEASES

BLOODLINE OF A SAVAGE 1&2
THESE VICIOUS STREETS
RELENTLESS GOON
RELENTLESS GOON 2
BY PRINCE A. TAUHID

THE BUTTERFLY MAFIA 1-3
BY FUMIYA PAYNE

A THUG'S STREET PRINCESS 1&2
BY MEESHA

CITY OF SMOKE 2
BY MOLOTTI

STEPPERS 1,2&3
BY KING RIO

THE LANE 1&2
BY KEN-KEN SPENCE

THUG OF SPADES 1&2
LOVE IN THE TRENCHES 2
BY COREY ROBINSON

TIL DEATH 3
BY ARYANNA

THE BIRTH OF A GANGSTER 4
BY DELMONT PLAYER

KILLA KOUNTY PART 5 | KHUFU

PRODUCT OF THE STREETS 1&2
BY DEMOND "MONEY" ANDERSON

NO TIME FOR ERROR
BY KEESE

MONEY HUNGRY DEMONS
BY TRANAY ADAMS

Coming Soon from Lock Down Publications/Ca$h Presents

IF YOU CROSS ME ONCE 6
ANGEL V
By Anthony Fields

IMMA DIE BOUT MINE 4&5
By Aryanna

A THUGS STREET PRINCESS 3
By Meesha

PRODUCT OF THE STREETS 3
By Demond Money Anderson

CORNER BOYS
By Corey Robinson

SON OF A DOPE FIEND 4
By Renta

THE MURDER QUEENS 6&7
By Michael Gallon

CITY OF SMOKE 3
By Molotti

BETRAYAL OF A G
By Ray Vinci

CONFESSIONS OF A DOPE BOY
By Nicholas Lock

THA TAKEOVER
By Keith Chandler

Available Now

RESTRAINING ORDER 1 & 2
By **CA$H & Coffee**

LOVE KNOWS NO BOUNDARIES 1-3
By **Coffee**

RAISED AS A GOON I, II, III & IV
BRED BY THE SLUMS I, II, III
BLAST FOR ME I & II
ROTTEN TO THE CORE I II III
A BRONX TALE I, II, III
DUFFLE BAG CARTEL I II III IV V VI
HEARTLESS GOON I II III IV V
A SAVAGE DOPEBOY I II
DRUG LORDS I II III
CUTTHROAT MAFIA I II
KING OF THE TRENCHES
By **Ghost**

LAY IT DOWN I & II
LAST OF A DYING BREED I II
BLOOD STAINS OF A SHOTTA I & II III
By **Jamaica**

LOYAL TO THE GAME I II III
LIFE OF SIN I, II III
By **TJ & Jelissa**

IF LOVING HIM IS WRONG…I & II
LOVE ME EVEN WHEN IT HURTS I II III
By **Jelissa**

KILLA KOUNTY PART 5 | KHUFU

BLOODY COMMAS I & II
SKI MASK CARTEL I, II & III
KING OF NEW YORK I II, III IV V
RISE TO POWER I II III
COKE KINGS I II III IV V
BORN HEARTLESS I II III IV
KING OF THE TRAP I II
By **T.J. Edwards**

WHEN THE STREETS CLAP BACK I & II III
THE HEART OF A SAVAGE I II III IV
MONEY MAFIA I II
LOYAL TO THE SOIL I II III
By **Jibril Williams**

A DISTINGUISHED THUG STOLE MY HEART I II &
III
LOVE SHOULDN'T HURT I II III IV
RENEGADE BOYS 1-4
PAID IN KARMA 1-3
SAVAGE STORMS 1-3
AN UNFORESEEN LOVE 1-3
BABY, I'M WINTERTIME COLD 1-3
A THUG'S STREET PRINCESS 1&2
By **Meesha**

A GANGSTER'S CODE 1-3
A GANGSTER'S SYN 1-3
THE SAVAGE LIFE 1-3
CHAINED TO THE STREETS 1-3
BLOOD ON THE MONEY 1-3
A GANGSTA'S PAIN 1-3
BEAUTIFUL LIES AND UGLY TRUTHS
CHURCH IN THESE STREETS
By **J-Blunt**

KILLA KOUNTY PART 5 | KHUFU

PUSH IT TO THE LIMIT
By **Bre' Hayes**

BLOOD OF A BOSS 1-5
SHADOWS OF THE GAME
TRAP BASTARD
By **Askari**

THE STREETS BLEED MURDER 1-3
THE HEART OF A GANGSTA 1-3
By **Jerry Jackson**

CUM FOR ME 1-8
An LDP Erotica Collaboration

BRIDE OF A HUSTLA 1-3
THE FETTI GIRLS 1-3
CORRUPTED BY A GANGSTA 1-4
BLINDED BY HIS LOVE
THE PRICE YOU PAY FOR LOVE 1-3
DOPE GIRL MAGIC 1-3
By **Destiny Skai**

WHEN A GOOD GIRL GOES BAD
By **Adrienne**

A KINGPIN'S AMBITION
A KINGPIN'S AMBITION II
I MURDER FOR THE DOUGH
By **Ambitious**

THE COST OF LOYALTY 1-3
By **Kweli**

A GANGSTER'S REVENGE 1-4
THE BOSS MAN'S DAUGHTERS 1-5
A SAVAGE LOVE 1&2
BAE BELONGS TO ME 1&2
A HUSTLER'S DECEIT 1-3
WHAT BAD BITCHES DO 1-3
SOUL OF A MONSTER 1-3
KILL ZONE
A DOPE BOY'S QUEEN 1-3
TIL DEATH 1-3
IMMA DIE BOUT MINE 1-3
By **Aryanna**

TRUE SAVAGE 1-7
DOPE BOY MAGIC 1-3
MIDNIGHT CARTEL 1-3
CITY OF KINGZ 1&2
NIGHTMARE ON SILENT AVE
THE PLUG OF LIL MEXICO 1&2
CLASSIC CITY
By **Chris Green**

A DOPEBOY'S PRAYER
By **Eddie "Wolf" Lee**

THE KING CARTEL 1-3
By **Frank Gresham**

THESE NIGGAS AIN'T LOYAL 1-3
By **Nikki Tee**

GANGSTA SHYT 1-3
By **CATO**

THE ULTIMATE BETRAYAL
By **Phoenix**

177

BOSS'N UP 1-3
By **Royal Nicole**

I LOVE YOU TO DEATH
By **Destiny J**

I RIDE FOR MY HITTA
I STILL RIDE FOR MY HITTA
By **Misty Holt**

LOVE & CHASIN' PAPER
By **Qay Crockett**

TO DIE IN VAIN
SINS OF A HUSTLA
By **ASAD**

BROOKLYN HUSTLAZ
By **Boogsy Morina**

BROOKLYN ON LOCK 1 & 2
By **Sonovia**

GANGSTA CITY
By **Teddy Duke**

A DRUG KING AND HIS DIAMOND 1-3
A DOPEMAN'S RICHES
HER MAN, MINE'S TOO 1&2
CASH MONEY HO'S
THE WIFEY I USED TO BE 1&2
PRETTY GIRLS DO NASTY THINGS
By **Nicole Goosby**

LIPSTICK KILLAH 1-3
CRIME OF PASSION 1-3
FRIEND OR FOE 1-3
By **Mimi**

TRAPHOUSE KING 1-3
KINGPIN KILLAZ 1-3
STREET KINGS 1&2
PAID IN BLOOD 1&2
CARTEL KILLAZ 1-3
DOPE GODS 1&2
By **Hood Rich**

STEADY MOBBN' 1-3
THE STREETS STAINED MY SOUL 1-3
By **Marcellus Allen**

WHO SHOT YA 1-3
SON OF A DOPE FIEND 1-3
HEAVEN GOT A GHETTO 1&2
SKI MASK MONEY 1&2
By **Renta**

GORILLAZ IN THE BAY 1-4
TEARS OF A GANGSTA 1/&2
3X KRAZY 1&2
STRAIGHT BEAST MODE 1&2
By **DE'KARI**

TRIGGADALE 1-3
MURDA WAS THE CASE 1-3
By **Elijah R. Freeman**

THE STREETS ARE CALLING
By **Duquie Wilson**

KILLA KOUNTY PART 5 | KHUFU

SLAUGHTER GANG 1-3
RUTHLESS HEART 1-3
By **Willie Slaughter**

GOD BLESS THE TRAPPERS 1-3
THESE SCANDALOUS STREETS 1-3
FEAR MY GANGSTA 1-5
THESE STREETS DON'T LOVE NOBODY 1-2
BURY ME A G 1-5
A GANGSTA'S EMPIRE 1-4
THE DOPEMAN'S BODYGAURD 1&2
THE REALEST KILLAZ 1-3
THE LAST OF THE OGS 1-3
By **Tranay Adams**

MARRIED TO A BOSS 1-3
By **Destiny Skai & Chris Green**

KINGZ OF THE GAME 1-7
CRIME BOSS 1-3
By **Playa Ray**

FUK SHYT
By **Blakk Diamond**

DON'T F#CK WITH MY HEART 1&2
By **Linnea**

ADDICTED TO THE DRAMA 1-3
IN THE ARM OF HIS BOSS
By **Jamila**

LOYALTY AIN'T PROMISED 1&2
By **Keith Williams**

KILLA KOUNTY PART 5 | KHUFU

YAYO 1-4
A SHOOTER'S AMBITION 1&2
BRED IN THE GAME
By **S. Allen**

TRAP GOD 1-3
RICH $AVAGE 1-3
MONEY IN THE GRAVE 1-3
CARTEL MONEY
By **Martell Troublesome Bolden**

FOREVER GANGSTA 1&2
GLOCKS ON SATIN SHEETS 1&2
By **Adrian Dulan**

TOE TAGZ 1-4
LEVELS TO THIS SHYT 1&2
IT'S JUST ME AND YOU
By **Ah'Million**

KINGPIN DREAMS 1-3
RAN OFF ON DA PLUG
By **Paper Boi Rari**

CONFESSIONS OF A GANGSTA 1-4
CONFESSIONS OF A JACKBOY 1-3
CONFESSIONS OF A HITMAN
By **Nicholas Lock**

I'M NOTHING WITHOUT HIS LOVE
SINS OF A THUG
TO THE THUG I LOVED BEFORE
A GANGSTA SAVED XMAS
IN A HUSTLER I TRUST
By **Monet Dragun**

QUIET MONEY 1-3
THUG LIFE 1-3
EXTENDED CLIP 1&2
A GANGSTA'S PARADISE
By **Trai'Quan**

CAUGHT UP IN THE LIFE 1-3
THE STREETS NEVER LET GO 1-3
By **Robert Baptiste**

NEW TO THE GAME 1-3
MONEY, MURDER & MEMORIES 1-3
By **Malik D. Rice**

CREAM 2-3
THE STREETS WILL TALK
By **Yolanda Moore**

LIFE OF A SAVAGE 1-4
A GANGSTA'S QUR'AN 1-4
MURDA SEASON 1-3
GANGLAND CARTEL 1-3
CHI'RAQ GANGSTAS 1-4
KILLERS ON ELM STREET 1-3
JACK BOYZ N DA BRONX 1-3
A DOPEBOY'S DREAM 1-3
JACK BOYS VS DOPE BOYS 1-3
COKE GIRLZ
COKE BOYS
SOSA GANG 1&2
BRONX SAVAGES
BODYMORE KINGPINS
BLOOD OF A GOON
By **Romell Tukes**

KILLA KOUNTY PART 5 | KHUFU

THE STREETS MADE ME 1-3
By **Larry D. Wright**

CONCRETE KILLA 1-3
VICIOUS LOYALTY 1-3
By **Kingpen**

THE ULTIMATE SACRIFICE 1-6
KHADIFI
IF YOU CROSS ME ONCE 1-3
ANGEL 1-4
IN THE BLINK OF AN EYE
By **Anthony Fields**

THE LIFE OF A HOOD STAR
By **Ca$h & Rashia Wilson**

THE STREETS WILL NEVER CLOSE 1-3
By **K'ajji**

NIGHTMARES OF A HUSTLA 1-3
By **King Dream**

HARD AND RUTHLESS 1&2
MOB TOWN 251
THE BILLIONAIRE BENTLEYS 1-3
REAL G'S MOVE IN SILENCE
By **Von Diesel**

GHOST MOB
By **Stilloan Robinson**

MOB TIES 1-6
SOUL OF A HUSTLER, HEART OF A KILLER 1-3
GORILLAZ IN THE TRENCHES
By **SayNoMore**

BODYMORE MURDERLAND 1-3
THE BIRTH OF A GANGSTER 1-4
By **Delmont Player**

FOR THE LOVE OF A BOSS 1&2
By **C. D. Blue**

KILLA KOUNTY 1-5
By **Khufu**

MOBBED UP 1-4
THE BRICK MAN 1-5
THE COCAINE PRINCESS 1-10
STEPPERS 1-3
SUPER GREMLIN 1-4
By **King Rio**

MONEY GAME 1&2
By **Smoove Dolla**

A GANGSTA'S KARMA 1-4
By **FLAME**

KING OF THE TRENCHES 1-3
By **GHOST & TRANAY ADAMS**

QUEEN OF THE ZOO 1&2
By **Black Migo**

GRIMEY WAYS 1-3
By **Ray Vinci**

XMAS WITH AN ATL SHOOTER
By **Ca$h & Destiny Skai**

KILLA KOUNTY PART 5 | KHUFU

KING KILLA 1&2
By **Vincent "Vitto" Holloway**

BETRAYAL OF A THUG 1&2
By **Fre$h**

THE MURDER QUEENS 1-5
By **Michael Gallon**

FOR THE LOVE OF BLOOD 1-4
By **Jamel Mitchell**

HOOD CONSIGLIERE 1&2
NO TIME FOR ERROR
By **Keese**

PROTÉGÉ OF A LEGEND 1&2
LOVE IN THE TRENCHES 1&2
By **Corey Robinson**

BORN IN THE GRAVE 1-3
CRIME PAYS
By **Self Made Tay**

MOAN IN MY MOUTH
By **XTASY**

TORN BETWEEN A GANGSTER AND A GENTLEMAN
By **J-BLUNT & Miss Kim**

LOYALTY IS EVERYTHING 1-3
CITY OF SMOKE 1&2
By **Molotti**

HERE TODAY GONE TOMORROW 1&2
By **Fly Rock**

WOMEN LIE MEN LIE 1-4
FIFTY SHADES OF SNOW 1-3
STACK BEFORE YOU SPLURGE
GIRLS FALL LIKE DOMINOES
NAÏVE TO THE STREETS
By **ROY MILLIGAN**

PILLOW PRINCESS
By **S. Hawkins**

THE BUTTERFLY MAFIA 1-3
SALUTE MY SAVAGERY 1&2
By **Fumiya Payne**

THE LANE 1&2
By Ken-Ken Spence

THE PUSSY TRAP 1-5
By **Nene Capri**

DIRTY DNA
By **Blaque**

SANCTIFIED AND HORNY
by **XTASY**

BOOKS BY LDP'S CEO, CA$H

TRUST IN NO MAN
TRUST IN NO MAN 2
TRUST IN NO MAN 3
BONDED BY BLOOD
SHORTY GOT A THUG
THUGS CRY
THUGS CRY 2
THUGS CRY 3
TRUST NO BITCH
TRUST NO BITCH 2
TRUST NO BITCH 3
TIL MY CASKET DROPS
RESTRAINING ORDER
RESTRAINING ORDER 2
IN LOVE WITH A CONVICT
LIFE OF A HOOD STAR
XMAS WITH AN ATL SHOOTER

www.ingramcontent.com/pod-product-compliance
Lightning Source LLC
Chambersburg PA
CBHW070519260626
47161CB00004B/1591